Carolyn J. Pollack

Heavens . . . There are so many people to thank for getting *Vendetta of Love* to the publishers that I hardly know where to start, but as I sit here writing this, a thought comes to mind that I work with two of the most amazing people. For starters, there's Jessica (and Nick Muchow), who agreed to be my Mackenzie Phillips (and Dean Ashleigh). Without them, I would have been stuck for characters for *Vendetta*'s cover. The fact that they are beautiful on the inside as well as the outside is an added bonus. They gave their time freely and without the slightest bit of hesitation. I remember nervously asking Jess if she'd consider posing for me, and the answer came back instantly, "Yes, I'll do it for you."

"Great," I said, "now all I need is a man to pose with you."

"No problem," she said. "My husband, Nick, will do it." And he did.

But then I think as great as it is that Jess and Nick agreed to pose for me, where would I be without someone to take the photos? That's where the talented Karen Ebert comes into the picture (pardon the pun). Karen is another selfless person who doesn't know her true worth as a photographer, and she is a very nice person to boot. Again, as with Jess, I approached Karen with a request to take the photographs I wanted for *Vendetta*, telling her what I had in mind; and I think when you see the photographs we chose, you will see that they speak for themselves. Karen took 199 photographs. It was so very difficult to choose from so many great pics.

So I'd like to say a very heartfelt thank you to these three people for helping me get *Vendetta of Love* to the publisher at long last. Thank you seems so little to say for the work they have put into this story. I might have created the words, but Jess, Nick, and Karen have helped to bring *Vendetta of Love* to life in a way I'm sure that you, the reader, will thoroughly enjoy.

CHAPTER ONE

"Why couldn't you have rented the house to a crotchety old maid, one who liked nothing better than to sit on her verandah and abuse everyone in the street as they went past?" Mackenzie asked, knowing that she was being totally unreasonable.

She could see the humour starting to build on her friend's face, so she tagged on, "No, I mean it. Anything would be better than the situation your moving is going to place me in. My god, Jazz, what were you and Rob thinking when you agreed to rent your house to that horrible man?"

A mischievous smile was starting to tug at the corners of Jazz's mouth. This was the absolute last straw. She was unable to stop the flow of laughter that bubbled up from within her. The thought of Mackenzie being daunted by her new neighbour was too hilarious to contemplate. Day after day, she stood in front of various classrooms full of reluctant students whose one aim in life, according to Jazz, was to make their teacher's life miserable; yet here she was, complaining about the presence of one mere male.

"Mackenzie, you're exaggerating. I've met the man, and he seemed very nice. In fact, I thought you'd think he was kind of cute."

It suddenly hit Mackenzie that this man's presence in the house next door wasn't the random choosing she'd thought it to be but a carefully orchestrated plan on the part of her soon-to-be ex-neighbour.

"Jazz, you didn't!" Mackenzie stared at her friend in horror as realisation started to set in. Surely, she hadn't planned this awful chain of events in the hope of getting her together with that awful man. The thought didn't bear thinking about, but it was the kind of warped idea that Jazz would come up with in order to get her friend fixed up as she was fond of telling Mackenzie.

"No, I didn't!"

Mackenzie threw her friend a look which clearly stated that she wasn't about to believe a single word of the explanation which was to follow.

"Honestly, Mac," Jazz continued, "I didn't, but I didn't think you'd protest this much. I thought you'd like having a neighbour that you had something in common with." Seeing the incredulous look on Mackenzie's face, Jazz tacked on, "You know, being a teacher and all, I must admit it did cross my mind that you might go out sometimes. I certainly didn't envisage World War III breaking out between the two of you or that our fence line would become the Great Wall of China or the Berlin Wall or whatever. Think of the great times we've had talking over the fence since we first arrived five years ago . . ." She looked across at her friend, wanting confirmation. "We'd work in our respective gardens, talking about anything and everything that came into our minds."

"Yes, but that was with you!" Mackenzie wailed. "I can't very well strike up a conversation with him, telling him that I thought the baker's buns looked extra good, can I?"

Jazz laughed. She knew she was going to miss these intimate conversations she shared with Mackenzie. She told her impishly, "Perhaps not, but you could tell him that his aren't too bad."

"I don't want a man in my life, remember?" Mackenzie told her friend as she abruptly stood up, not wanting to pursue this particular conversation any further. She was happy with her lot in life. She didn't want, or need, the hassles that would arise from having a man in her life again, although she had to admit that there were times when she missed the physical relationship she'd enjoyed with Steve. Her face clouded as she thought of her late husband. The words rang in her ears—"late husband." It was still so hard to believe. Steve had been dead for more than three years now.

"Hey, where did you go?" Jazz wanted to know as she slowly pushed herself up from the verandah step.

"What?" Mackenzie asked, looking at her friend. She was still not clearly back in the land of the living.

"Just as I thought," Jazz accused, pointing a finger towards her friend.

"Mackenzie, I know you loved Steve dearly, but it's time to let him go. You've buried yourself along with him, and that's not good. You're still young and alive. It's time you got on with your life."

"Jazz, please, let's not start this again." Mackenzie attempted a smile that barely lifted the corners of her mouth. It certainly didn't reach her lovely brown eyes.

"Okay, you win for now, but one day, a man is going to come along and knock you flying off that pedestal of yours. I just hope you're going to be ready for it when it happens." Jazz was genuinely concerned about her friend's welfare. She'd been out with the occasional man since the death of her husband, but none of them had held her interest for longer than one or two outings. It was just so wrong. It filled her with dismay to see someone as beautiful as Mackenzie throwing herself away on a memory.

Mackenzie's beauty wasn't just on the outside. She was one of those rare people who cared about everyone. Just once, Jazz would like to see someone give some of that special love back.

"The moment it happens, you'll be the first to know, alright?" Mackenzie told her as she tried to hold back the slight grin that was threatening to break the serious composure of her fair features.

Her complete lack of enthusiasm was evident because Jazz responded smugly, "You can laugh now, but you just wait until it happens. They say love can hit you like a bolt out of the blue."

Mackenzie's nonchalant gaze took in the cloudless blue sky before looking once more at her friend. "Well, not today, my friend, the horizon looks perfectly clear. Now come on, Rob will think you've forgotten about him . . . or had you?" Mackenzie asked casually, knowing full well that this wasn't the case. Jazz and Rob had a wonderful marriage; as a couple, they were completely suited.

Jazz threw her friend a glance that told her their conversation was by no means over, but for now, she'd have to put it on hold. "No, I hadn't forgotten, it's wonderful to know that there's a big, sexy man waiting at home for me. Has it been so long that you've forgotten?"

"Hello . . . Would you be Mrs. Phillips, by any chance? Hello." Mackenzie wasn't to know what a fetching picture she made sitting there as she was, framed in the open doorway. Strands of tawny brown hair had escaped from the brightly coloured band she wore to keep the errant strands in place. They tumbled down her back in vibrant disarray, catching shards of light from the late morning sun as it made its way slowly across a cloudless blue sky. Nothing seemed to be in a hurry on this lazy Saturday morning, least of all this attractive young woman sitting before him. She seemed to be oblivious to his presence. He was about to try again when she finally seemed to come to life. Well, to notice him anyway.

Slowly coming out of her trancelike state, Mackenzie stared uncomprehendingly up at the individual who stood before her. She'd literally been miles away, thinking once again of the couple she'd so recently been forced to say her good-byes to. As her mind cleared of the reminiscent fog that had enshrouded it, she began to focus on the man who was lounging casually against the railing on her back steps. Heavens, how long had he been standing there, waiting for her to acknowledge his presence?

He had a distinct advantage, standing over her the way he was. He was very tall, Mackenzie noticed. She'd be dwarfed even if she was standing against him. He'd have to be well over six feet tall, Mackenzie surmised from where she sat, sprawled across the doorway in her usual unladylike position.

"Um, I'm sorry. What did you say?" If she had her wits about her, she'd have been horrified by her apparent lack of concern for her immediate safety. For instance, what was a strange man doing in her back yard? Where had he come from, and more importantly, who was he? But none of these questions made their way into her befuddled brain as Mackenzie continued to stare blankly up at him.

"I asked if you were Mrs. Phillips?" his voice had a deep timbre to it, and in any other circumstances, Mackenzie felt she'd have loved to listen to him, but for now, she felt it, and he was an intrusion to her badly needed privacy. She'd slept badly last night and, after a lot of restless tossing and turning, had decided to get out of bed. As the first rays of the morning sun had touched the mountains, she'd gone for a long walk only to find that she'd taken her problems along with her. There was a special magic at this time of the morning, when everything was new and ready to start another day, but this morning had been different. She knew that today was the start of a new era.

Upon reaching home, she'd initiated a vigorous exercise routine, hoping that the strenuous workout would help her sleep; but here it was several hours later, and she was still wide awake. Usually by this time of a Saturday morning, she was up and about, doing all of the household chores that were put off during the week because of her busy work schedule; but today for some reason, her vigor had deserted her. She still wore her skimpy red and white crop top and her body-hugging black tights that she'd exercised in. She'd kicked off her shoes and peeled off one sock, the other one was still on her foot.

Oh well, she thought despondently, *if people choose to visit me unannounced, they have to expect what they get.* She just didn't feel like doing anything, and now this man had arrived to interrupt her reverie.

Remnants of some toast and an empty coffee mug sat forlornly on the floor beside her, evidence that she'd been sitting there for quite a while. Also, there was a trail of ants busily at work, carrying off the toast crumbs that Mackenzie had scattered on the steps for them to eat.

In spite of herself, her brain started to register that the stranger standing in front of her was no ordinary male. He'd straightened up, and Mackenzie realised her first assumption about his height had to be correct. She was starting to notice other things about him as well, but her thoughts were interrupted when he asked yet again, "Are you Mrs. Phillips or not? I was told by a neighbour that she lived here." She could tell from the tone of his voice that he was quickly losing his patience. He'd actually started to look past her into the house, probably hoping to find someone who would at least answer his questions.

How rude, Mackenzie thought to herself as she took an extra few seconds to look at him before answering. "Yes, I'm Mrs. Phillips. What do you want?" She knew her tone could have been a lot friendlier, but she didn't care. Who did he think he was anyway?

"Keys?" he said matter-of-factly, ignoring Mackenzie's unfriendly manner. "I've come for the keys."

This just wasn't Mackenzie's day. She stared up at him blankly, not having the slightest idea what he was talking about. "Keys," she repeated, stupidly, "what keys?"

"The . . . keys . . . to . . . the . . . house . . . next . . . door," he told her slowly, putting emphasis on every word as he indicated with a turn of his head towards the house that had been vacated only yesterday by her friends, Jazz and Rob.

Mackenzie glared up at him with an expression that was full of malice. There was no reason for him to treat her like she was a moron, but still she wasn't forthcoming with an answer to his repeated question and so just sat there continuing to stare up at him.

"Do you have the keys," he asked again, "to the house next door, or not?"

He was staring at her with something akin to anger in his cold, brown eyes. His dark brows were drawn together as he studied her intently, obviously waiting for some kind of an answer.

"Yes, I have them," Mackenzie flung at him, not caring that she was being unreasonably rude. The only thought that was whirling through her brain was that this insufferable man was to be her new neighbour. Mackenzie had told Jazz this would happen when she'd first been told about their forthcoming move. Now it looked as if her worst fears had come to pass.

"At last! Now we're getting somewhere. Could I have them, please? It would be nice if I could move in some time this year if that's at all possible." The sarcasm wasn't wasted on Mackenzie as she waspishly glared up at him, letting him know in no uncertain terms that she didn't appreciate being the beneficiary of his glib tongue.

Mackenzie was conscious of his gaze on her as he continued to look down at her. His eyes were unreadable brown slits that seemed to be looking into her very soul. "That was uncalled for," she spat back at him as she rose unceremoniously to walk inside to fetch the keys to Jazz and Rob's house. She was back in less than a minute, holding the keys out to him in a manner which was neither friendly nor welcoming.

"Here," she said, thrusting the keys at him. She wanted this man off her property and out of her sight, and the sooner, the better.

Glittering dark eyes raked her from the top of her head to the tip of her toes as she stood on the step looking down at him. She was under no illusions that he saw her as someone to be avoided at all costs. Well, that suited her just fine; she wouldn't have an ounce of trouble complying with his unspoken wishes.

They were saved from any further confrontation by the sudden appearance of a brunette woman who was making her way towards them from the direction of the other house. She smiled pleasantly at them both before asking the man, who was obviously her companion, the question that had been continuously thrust at her for the last few minutes.

"There you are. I was beginning to think you were lost. Did you get the keys?"

Mackenzie didn't know why, but she suddenly felt an overwhelming desire to burst out laughing. Somehow it sounded extremely funny to hear someone else starting to ask for the keys. She had the good sense to stifle the laugh, before it had a chance to bubble up from within her throat.

His reaction was to scowl at them both, before ungraciously grabbing the offered keys from her outstretched hand.

"Thank you," he told her through clenched teeth, and then he was turning abruptly away, much to the astonishment and confusion of his companion, who had no choice but to blindly follow him back across the short expanse of grass which led around the side of the house and eventually out of sight. Mackenzie could just imagine how their conversation was progressing. He'd be telling his companion about his zany new neighbour.

A spontaneous, mad impulse grabbed Mackenzie, and on the spur of the moment, she blurted out gaily to the retreating figures, "Bye for now, glad I could be of help. Come around anytime." She threw the retreating figures a gay little wave, safe in the knowledge that he wasn't going to see her madcap antics.

At first, she thought her taunt was to be ignored, but at the last moment, before turning the corner of her house, he glanced back, throwing her a look of pure malice, letting her know in no uncertain terms that he wasn't about to play these childish games with her. His look also conveyed another message, which left Mackenzie feeling acutely vulnerable. She didn't know why exactly, but she had the distinct feeling that he wasn't finished with her yet.

Mackenzie thought sadly about the woman who'd been with him. It was sad how some women couldn't see past a man's good looks, to see what was beneath the skin, what was in his innermost thoughts and heart.

They were probably going out, or perhaps they were even married. Jazz hadn't mentioned a wife in her constant ramblings about him, but then perhaps he hadn't told her friend everything about his personal life. She was, after all, only his landlady, not his priest or confessor.

She had to grudgingly admit to herself that this particular man was very good looking. When she'd finally become aware of his presence, her mind must have unconsciously gathered the physical information about him because she found she now had not the slightest bit of trouble in conjuring up a perfect mental picture of him, one that she could bring forth to investigate at her leisure.

She'd already acknowledged the fact that he was tall, but she now recalled that he had dark blonde hair, which had a tendency to fall across his wide forehead. He'd kept brushing the dark blonde locks out of the way with a hand that looked strong and masculine. He'd also had a habit of lifting an eyebrow when he'd been trying to make her listen to him. Mackenzie remembered he'd used this personal trait on several occasions throughout their brief conversation. His eyes were a rich, chocolate brown and were protected by thick dark brows, which had come together in a scowl when he'd showed his displeasure at the taunt she'd thrown at him on his departure. He had a wonderful physique, which had been accentuated by the clothes he'd been wearing. He had broad shoulders that had tapered down to slim hips, where faded blue jeans had hung snugly but not tightly, going on to cover legs that were long and straight. A casual aqua blue top had enhanced the lightly tanned skin of his face and neck. Mackenzie remembered seeing a small amount of fine, silky, black chest hair protruding out over the top of his shirt where he'd opted to leave the uppermost buttons undone. She doubted if he carried an ounce of spare flesh on that all-together too perfect body. All in all, his general appearance had made a very sound impression on her if she'd only realised it at the time.

Mackenzie slowly shook her head, trying to rid herself of the image which seemed to have ingrained itself onto her memory. Picking up the remnants of her breakfast, she made her way inside, kicking the door closed with her foot. She didn't want to be a silent witness to his perusal of Jazz and Rob's house nor did she want to have to look at him again in the near future. Let him show his friend over the house without her having to observe them from her position on her back steps.

This was probably the way it was going to be from now on, she mused as she set about cleaning up her breakfast mess.

She thought of the small parcel of land that separated the two houses from each other and forlornly registered in her mind that although there was a fence dividing the two properties, both Jazz and herself had freely commuted between the two allotments as they'd seen fit. This too would now be at an end. In fact, it had already stopped. Mackenzie couldn't see herself running over to tell him about the happenings in her life. *Yes*, she thought yet again, *the brunette woman was welcome to him*. If she never laid eyes on him again, it would be too soon, way too soon.

Anyway, what business is it of mine? she mused to herself as she made her way down the short hallway that led to her bedroom.

Mackenzie's restless night was finally catching up with her. *Perhaps if I lay down for a while, I might feel a little better*, she thought dispiritedly. She was definitely not herself that much was true. She certainly wasn't the type of person who went around abusing people, but she stubbornly told herself that he'd deserved the treatment he'd received from her. It wasn't her fault that she hadn't heard his approach. Her mouth set stubbornly as she thought back over the events of their brief encounter. *Yes*, she told herself, with a surety that sounded almost convincing to her ears, *it was definitely his fault*.

Once in her room, Mackenzie started to peel off the clothes she'd donned to exercise in. She stepped out of them before walking over to the built-in cupboard which took up one entire wall of the bedroom. Her bedroom was simple as was the rest of the house. At the present time, it suited her needs to live here, then she thought of recent events, and her mouth straightened into a thin line. She'd promised herself she wasn't going to dwell on the past, and yet here she was, about to go on another mind-bender about her lost relationship with Steve.

She had the honesty to admit to herself that when it came to members of the opposite sex, her usually excellent judgment had a habit of leaving her high and dry and always alone.

She stifled a yawn as she dragged her weary body into the bathroom. She caught a glimpse of herself in the mirror as she headed out the bedroom door. Her reflection pulled her up short as she turned over in her mind the words that men usually said to her when they were on their crusade, which they fervently hoped would eventually lead them to her bed. This was a crusade which always failed.

Mackenzie had heard it so many times before. It was the same old line told, told, and retold again. "You're beautiful, Mackenzie." "You have a terrific body, Mackenzie." "Please, Mackenzie, let's make love. I promise you won't regret it." Just once she'd like to meet a man who saw her as a person in her own right and not as a sexual object to be used and then casually thrown away like a piece of used paper. She was sick and tired of fighting off men who couldn't get their minds above their belt buckle. Steve hadn't been like that.

The cool jets of water from the shower cooled her down, both physically and mentally. She resolved to be a better judge of character when next she chose to accept an invitation from a member of the opposite sex.

She spent the rest of the day lounging lazily around the house. She knew she should be tackling the large pile of papers which she'd specifically brought home with the intention of marking, but the thought of sitting down at the table and actually making a start on them filled her with instant disdain. *Anyway,* she told herself sadly, *I can do them tomorrow. I'm going to have a lot of empty tomorrows from now on.*

The insistent ringing of the telephone brought Mackenzie out of a dreamless sleep. She stumbled out of bed, kicking her toe on a chair in the process, wondering who in blazes could be phoning her at this godforsaken time of night. Turning on the light as she passed it, Mackenzie glanced at the small clock on the kitchen wall, which indicated to her that it was only eight o'clock in the evening.

"Hello," she mumbled into the mouthpiece, not really caring how she sounded to the person on the other end of the line. Let them make of it what they would.

A gentle laugh filled her ear as her caller expressed her thoughts. "Heavens, are you that bored without me that you have to retire to bed this early? Don't tell me I woke you up?"

"Jazz, hi, how are you?" Mackenzie could feel her lethargic mood melting away as she heard the cheerful voice of her friend. She smiled into the phone; this was just what she needed. Here was just the right person to talk to about her awful new neighbour, and who better to tell her troubles to than the very person who had inadvertently placed her in this horrible position?

Over an hour later, Mackenzie sat in her lounge room nursing a cup of coffee. Jazz had told her that she'd be coming up to Rocky in a few weeks time to tie up some loose ends. It sounded like Jazz and Rob had settled into their new home. Mackenzie still found it hard to accept that her best friend in the whole world now lived in another part of the state. Tears came unbidden into her soft brown eyes as she thought over the events of the day. Her bottom lip quivered, and she made a halfhearted attempt to stem the flow of tears, wiping them away with the back of her hand.

Her stomach started rumbling, reminding her that she hadn't eaten since early that morning. *A light snack might perk me up*, she thought miserably as she made her way across to the kitchen, turning on the television as she did so. She didn't keep a lot of food in the refrigerator, choosing instead to shop at regular intervals, so she wasn't surprised to see that when she opened the refrigerator door, there wasn't anything very appetising to take her fancy. In the end, she settled for some carrot sticks, some green beans, and some celery sticks that looked like they'd seen better days.

She found a small can of pumpkin soup tucked away in the back of the cupboard and, once heated, added the contents to her rather unappetising meal of raw vegetables.

Great, she lamented to herself as she crunched dejectedly on the last piece of carrot. *I know I was thinking of losing a few kilograms, but this is ridiculous.*

It wasn't that she wanted or really needed to lose weight so much as to control how her present weight was distributed. The exercises she did helped to keep her physically fit and trim. She was proud of her figure, so why shouldn't she work at trying to keep it?

Mackenzie walked back into her bedroom, stopping only when she stood in front of the full-length mirror that comprised the doors of the wardrobe. Dressed in skimpy underwear as she was, her view of her body wasn't restricted, and so she was able to study her reflection more closely.

She'd always thought she was way too tall for a female. Standing at five foot nine inches in her stocking feet, she'd always wished she was shorter. She remembered she'd always towered over the boys at school when she'd been growing up and had been the recipient of way too many tall jokes; some of them had hurt her terribly. Her mother had always told her to carry her height with pride, telling her that it would one day prove to be an asset, not a hindrance. Mackenzie was reluctant to believe her, both then and now, but at least she'd learned to live with it. As for her figure, she supposed it wasn't too bad. Her breasts were average, neither being too big nor too small. If she was to be honest with herself, she would have admitted to having a more than adequate figure that was very much in proportion and that she didn't need to lose those few extra kilograms that she was always going on about. In fact, if she were to lose any weight, she'd start to look gaunt, but she was being too stubborn to admit that, even to herself.

She had long, shapely legs which seemed to attract appreciative glances from the males of the species and looks of envy from a lot of the females. She found herself wondering if her new neighbour would find her legs attractive then immediately chastised herself for the thought, unable to think why such a thought would come unbidden into her mind. He'd be the last man she'd find attractive. He wasn't even her type. She conjured up a mental picture of him, remembering how he'd looked that morning as he'd stared up at her from the bottom of her back steps.

She knew it would be useless for her to go back to bed, for she was now wide awake; and glancing at the clock, she saw it was only 9:15 p.m. Perhaps she could watch something on television, but after a quick flick through the channels, she couldn't see anything that interested her enough to want to sit down and watch. She was feeling bored and could think of nothing to do that would fill the empty void. The evening stretched ahead of her like an unwelcome visitor.

She thought about going for a walk but quickly changed her mind when she heard some of the neighbourhood dogs starting up a chorus of barking. It was one thing putting up with dogs barking at her during the daylight hours, but she was darned if she was going to risk an attack this late at night.

After going through a number of scenario's in her mind, which would keep her occupied for the remainder of the evening, she finally decided she'd answer some long overdue letters to various members of her family and one or two absent friends. As she settled herself down at the kitchen table, she thought sadly how much her life had changed over the past three years since Steve's death. Here it was the shank of the evening, and she had nothing better to do than to sit and write letters. Other young people her age would be out enjoying themselves or at least spending their time in the company of a loved one. Her thoughts turned unbidden to her new neighbor, and she immediately censured herself, surprised at the clarity of the image that came into her mind.

"Oh, Steve!" she exclaimed, not for the first time since her husband's untimely death. "Why did you have to die?" A single tear ran silently down her cheek before she angrily wiped it away with the back of her hand.

Her letters were usually written hastily on scraps of paper or on postcards which depicted scenic locations in and around the Rockhampton area, but tonight, she decided she'd use the notepaper which had been a present from her mother, probably as a gentle prompt for Mackenzie to take a little more care or time with her letters to her family.

She knew her mother, especially, would appreciate a letter from her only daughter. It wasn't that she didn't keep in touch, she did; but she had a bad habit of telephoning from work whenever she had a spare minute, and those calls were usually hindered by interruptions of every kind. If she was to analyse her behavior, she'd be surprised to realise that she did this as a form of protection. It created a barrier which couldn't be penetrated because of her work environment. Her parents, along with everyone else, thought it was time she moved on and exorcised the ghost of her dead husband.

A few minutes later, Mackenzie was totally engrossed in her letter writing. She had a lot to tell her parents, and the words just seemed to flow onto the page. Her thoughts tumbled out faster than she could get them onto paper. She didn't notice the passing of time or how many pages she filled. It was good to get everything out of her system, and it also brought her parents up to date on every detail of their daughter's life. She knew they worried about her living so far away from home as she did, but they trusted her to make the right decisions in her life. Besides, they knew enough not to voice their concerns too vehemently. Mackenzie could be very stubborn, and if pushed, she had a tendency to dig in her heels, even when this course of action was detrimental or at cross purposes with anything she really wanted or needed. This trait, her mother vouchsafed, came from her father. Being wise parents, they knew that if she was left alone long enough, she usually made the right decisions concerning any course of action she was about to undertake.

It was some time later when she finally put down her pen. She had a crick in her neck which she tried unsuccessfully to rub away. She wasn't able to manipulate her fingers in a way that eased the stubborn ache. Unfolding herself from her chair, she stood up gingerly and began a series of stretches which had always helped to ease her tension in the past. The exercise worked to a small degree, but Mackenzie knew she needed to soak in a nice hot bath to feel completely free of the nagging ache which held her body captive.

First, she decided she'd make herself a hot drink. At least she knew she had some teabags and some powdered milk. She resolved that after work on Monday, she'd have to do some shopping and get some real food; she was beginning to feel like old Mother Hubbard.

Her padded footsteps echoed on the polished wood as she made her way down the hallway towards the bathroom. She was more than ready for that hot bath now. She had some lovely orange scented bath crystals, which she decided she'd add to the water. Stepping out of her underwear, she turned both taps on full blast before going to the cupboard to fetch the crystals. They smelled so lovely; their aroma filled the room as she lavishly sprinkled them into the hot water which was steadily filling the tub. She breathed in deeply as she made her way into her bedroom to fetch her night attire and some clean underwear. She spied a magazine lying on the floor beside her bed and bent down to pick it up, deciding that now would be a good time to browse through the glossy pages while she lay in the bath. There were one or two articles which she'd wanted to read. Her thoughts were interrupted as her brain registered the loud rushing of water, which could be heard coming from the bathroom.

On closer inspection, Mackenzie saw that her assumption had been correct. Hot water was gushing out of the tap at an alarming rate. "What the hell!" she exclaimed as she took in the scene before her. "Great, just great. This is all I needed to make my day complete."

When she tried to stop the torrent of water from rushing out of the tap, she found she was unable to. Nothing worked, and to make matters worse, the water was now dangerously close to the rim of the bathtub. Knowing she had to get the plug out before water started to run everywhere, she cautiously put her hand into the water but found that it was way too hot. If she tried to pull out the plug her whole arm would be scalded. She'd have to find another way to remove the damn thing, but she'd better be quick as the water was now lapping the top of the bathtub. Trying the tap one last time did nothing, and she cursed mildly as she frantically tried to think of another way to remove the plug. *One thing's for sure*, she thought, *after this, I'm going to put a chain on the damn thing, so I can pull it out without fear of burning my hand off.* She needed something to pry the plug out. But what could she use? What would work? *A coat hanger*, she thought wildly as she ran into her room where she grabbed a metal hanger from the cupboard, not heeding the clothes which fell to the floor. She'd worry about them later.

A frantic few minutes were lost as Mackenzie tried to fashion the top of the hanger into a hook. It was a few minutes in which the bath water actually started to flow over the top of the tub and onto the floor, where Mackenzie was standing.

The water had lost some of its heat. "Thank goodness for small mercies," Mackenzie muttered to herself as she stood in the puddle of water forming at her feet. *If this wasn't so serious, it could be funny*, Mackenzie thought as she finally looped the hastily made hook through the top of the plug, thus successfully pulling the stopper from the drain hole. *Here I am, completely naked, trying to save my house from flooding.* The thought brought a small smile to her lips. This is one story which wouldn't be told in the staffroom on Monday morning.

Although Mackenzie had removed the plug, the water wasn't draining away fast enough, and water still continued to spew forth into the bathtub. Mackenzie was perplexed and was momentarily at a loss, not knowing what to do next. The bathroom floor was awash, and Mackenzie grabbed towels from the cupboard, laying them down on the floor, hoping they'd soak up the excess water, but she could soon see that this was a solution which wasn't going to work. The water had to be stopped. But how? She couldn't let it run like this for the rest of the night. Then she remembered the water main, which was situated in the front yard; the one that was partially buried. There was no other way around it; she was going to have to go outside and turn the water to the house off. This thought filled her with trepidation as she thought of the creepy crawlies which inhabited her yard during the hours of darkness. The last thing she wanted to do was to grope around in the dark, looking for some damn water main.

Mackenzie could see that there wasn't going to be another course of action for her to take because the towels she'd laid on the floor earlier were now completely waterlogged. Water was now seeping out into the hallway. It would only be a matter of time before the whole house was flooded

Quickly putting on her bra and panties, she ran to the laundry cupboard to grab a torch, only to find that the batteries were flat. "Great, what a day this has turned out to be," she muttered to herself. Not only did she not have a torch, but she knew the outside light had blown, making it impossible for her to see what she was doing. It looked like she was going to have to grope around in the dark, looking for the water main. She only hoped that when she did locate it, it was free from any spiders or bugs, which might have made their home within the dark depths.

Then another thought struck her. What if there were frogs! She hated to admit it even to herself, but she was terrified of frogs. Everyone else seemed to think of this creature as a cute, green, croaking bundle of joy, but not Mackenzie. Her brothers had introduced her to frogs at a very tender age by putting one down her back as a joke. Mackenzie remembered how she'd reacted to the harmless prank. She shuddered as memories came flooding back to tease her. She'd screamed, wanting the squirming, startled animal away from her skin. To this day, her brothers teased her about her reaction to their joke. Every year on her birthday, as well as the other gifts she received from them, she'd be given a statue of a frog. She now had quite a collection of the little green monsters on display to taunt her.

If only she could turn the damn tap off. She went back to give the tap a final twist, hoping against hope that this time, the torrent would stop. The water was still gushing out at an alarming rate, not stopping by even a drop; but now at least it was cold. That meant all of her hot water was gone. Great, that meant that she was going to have to venture into the shed which housed the hot water system and turn it off as well. Heaven only knew what sort of nasties lived in there during the night. She shuddered at the thought.

Her mind returned to the present as she grimly opened the front door to cautiously peer out into the darkness.

"Well, I might as well get this over with," she told herself dejectedly as she headed down the front steps. The only thing she knew for sure was that the water main was at the front of the house on the left hand side, near the border between her house and Jazz's place or rather his house. She corrected herself miserably.

She felt a momentary spurt of anger against her friend, thinking that if she and Rob were still here, she could have called out to Rob who would have fixed everything up in a jiffy.

It took Mackenzie a few moments to locate the rectangular plastic cover which indicated the position of the water main. It was smaller than she remembered, but then it wasn't something that she'd normally paid a lot of attention to in the past. There was just enough room for her to put her hand into the hole and turn the tap off. Even though she knew it had to be done, Mackenzie hesitated before opening the lid. She could hear the water running into the bath from here, so she knew she had no other course of action but to turn it off. *If I let it go, anything could happen and probably would,* she thought grimly to herself.

The cover was heavier than she thought, and she pried it opened slowly, revealing a black hole which Mackenzie couldn't see into. The blackness worried her more than she cared to admit. Also, there were rustling noises in her near vicinity which she fervently hoped weren't being made by frogs. She looked around her, suppressing a shudder as she did so. She looked back into the hole, knowing she had to do it. There was no other way. *What if there's something down there*, she thought, *a spider or something and I disturb it? Some of those spiders can inflict a nasty bite. What if I get bitten?*

"Well, that's just a chance you'll have to take, isn't it?" she told herself sternly as she slowly lowered her hand into the black void which housed the water main. Her hand struck dirt sooner than she expected, and she jumped back in fright, withdrawing it quickly at the unexpected contact. *How could that be?* she thought to herself. *I'm sure this is the water main to the house.* Then it struck her—the tap was buried. She'd have to dig it out. Her prying fingers tried to push the dirt aside, but still the tap didn't surface. She'd have to grab a spoon or something to loosen the buildup of soil.

Returning a few minutes later with a spoon and a fork, she soon had the tap uncovered, but was still unable to turn the errant faucet off. It seemed to be stuck, and no amount of force seemed to budge it. *Perhaps if I dig it out a bit more, it will move*, she thought.

Five minutes later saw her no closer to her goal, and she threw the spoon away in frustration, only to immediately regret her impulsive action as she heard the steady gush of water still coming from inside the house.

"You stupid idiot! Now you'll have to find the blasted thing," she admonished herself severely as she started to crawl around in the darkness, looking for the spoon which at the moment felt more like looking for a needle in a haystack.

She was concentrating on the task at hand and failed to notice that she had a witness to her midnight sojourn. Someone was standing in the shadows, watching her progress with undisguised interest.

Her new neighbour had walked in to the kitchen for a drink of water, not bothering to turn on any of the house lights, when he'd heard a noise in the front yard. He'd been thinking that perhaps he'd find a dog or some other animal on the premises and had cautiously walked outside to investigate. The one thing in the world which he hadn't expected to find was someone digging in his front yard. Well, the yard next door to be precise. He was about to make his presence known when the moon came out from behind the clouds, presenting him with a view of a nearly naked woman. All she had on was her underwear or near enough. He stopped dead in his tracks as he tried to rationalise the scene transpiring before him. What in heaven's name was going on?

On closer inspection, he recognised the woman he'd spoken to earlier in the day. This confirmed his first impression—she was totally mad. Too bad too because she wasn't all that bad to look at even by moonlight. He continued staring, taking in the view which was before him. He wasn't sure what he should do. Should he stay or go? For all he knew, he could be interrupting some sort of ritual. It was then that the sound of running water reached his ears, and everything magically fell into place, making all of the pieces of this particular puzzle fit together perfectly.

"You look like you could use a hand," he said as he slowly approached Mackenzie.

Mackenzie's first impression of her knight in shining armour wasn't a pleasant one. She'd been completely absorbed in trying to find the spoon she'd flung into the darkness. Hearing a strange voice in the middle of the night was frightening enough, but to look up and find the owner of that voice bearing down on her was more than she could take, and to make matters worse, he was half naked.

She couldn't remember a time when she'd ever been as frightened as she was at this particular time in her life. Her initial reaction was to scream, which she did. Her instincts told her she should try to run, to get away from this potential threat to herself, but she was at a distinct disadvantage, being on all fours on the ground. She tried to get up but found that because she'd been crouched for so long, she was unable to run. The only thing she accomplished with any success was to fall in a heap at the intruder's feet.

"Stay away from me or you'll be sorry," she cautioned, holding the kitchen fork out in front of her defensively. Her heart was beating rapidly from fright as she peered into the darkness, trying to get a better look at her would-be assailant.

"What will you do if I don't, eat me?" came the instant reply from out of the darkness. The voice held a hint of amusement as if the owner found the whole situation highly entertaining.

A hand reached out towards her through the darkness, and Mackenzie cringed away in fear. "It's alright, Mrs. Phillips," the voice said in a more reassuring manner. "You don't have to be afraid of me. I'm your new neighbour, Dean Ashleigh. I was getting a glass of water when I heard a noise. I came out to investigate and found you digging. By the sound of the water running inside your house, you need to stop the flow. You've probably broken a washer. It will have to be replaced before the water can be turned back on."

"I can't get it to stop," Mackenzie flung at him. "The tap's stuck." She indicated the offending piece of equipment with a turn of her head. She felt ridiculous sitting here at his feet like he was some kind of god who was waiting to be worshipped.

He still held his hand out towards her, and Mackenzie knew she had no choice but to take the help he was offering. For some strange reason, she felt like crying. Why was this happening? And to make matters worse, she was in her underwear, for god's sake. It was all very disconcerting to say the least. She was sure that in years to come, she'd be able to look back on this terrible, disastrous night and laugh about it, but she thought ruefully that time would be a long time coming.

"Come on, up you get," he told her as if he was talking to a child. He unceremoniously yanked her to her feet before turning away to give his undivided attention to the task at hand.

Now that his attention was diverted elsewhere and away from her, Mackenzie felt free to take a closer look at him. Even by moonlight, she could see the muscles in his back ripple as he worked at freeing the offending tap. Like herself, he was scantily dressed; but in his case, he was wearing what Mackenzie perceived to be a pair of shorts. Her earlier assumptions regarding his physique seemed to be true. He did have a nice body.

"There, that seems to have done the trick." He tossed over his shoulder before standing up, turning in the process so that he now stood facing her.

Mackenzie had been so preoccupied with her thoughts of him that she hadn't noticed that the distant roar of running water had stopped.

"Um . . . yes," she said quickly, latching on to the first words she could think of to say to him, "Um . . . thank you for your help," she tagged on as an afterthought. She felt perfectly ridiculous standing here like this. How did one make an exit in these circumstances? Her book of etiquette hadn't mentioned what a young lady should do when she was confronted by a man while both were only partially dressed? Did you draw attention to the fact, or did you carry on as if it was a common occurrence to be caught in this situation in the middle of the night?

"Well . . . I'd better go in . . . I've got some cleaning up to do before I can go to bed . . . Thanks again," she said as she turned away from him, not really sure of what she should be doing.

"That's okay," he answered, then added glibly, "Glad I could be of help. Just call me anytime." He watched her walk away, finding the back view was nearly as good as the view from the front.

Mackenzie turned at his last remark to look at him, not knowing how to react to this piece of information. Her words to him from the morning came back to haunt her. She was sure that he was remembering also.

It was only once she was inside that she remembered she hadn't turned off the hot water system, which meant she'd have to go outside again. Blast, she hoped he'd gone. Perhaps if she stole a look through the curtains in the kitchen, she'd be able to tell.

It seemed to be clear outside, so presumably, he'd gone back to his own home. Mackenzie turned, her intention being to go back outside. She was appalled to see him standing in her open doorway, watching her intently. His look was inscrutable with the exception of a small pulse, which seemed to be beating in the small of his neck. She gasped involuntarily, taking a step backwards which brought her flush up against the kitchen sink.

"What . . . what do you want?" She was still holding the fork in her hands, twisting it around nervously as she spoke.

He noticed this and allowed himself a small grin before explaining to her slowly. "It occurred to me you might like to clean up, but as you're now without water, it might be a bit hard to do. If you like, you can use the shower at my place."

"Oh! Well . . . um . . . I suppose I am a bit dirty." Mackenzie looked down at herself and found she was covered with dirt and bits of dry grass. *God, will this night never end*, she thought to herself.

"I'm sorry, but I have to be rude and ask . . ." *Oh hell,* Mackenzie moaned, *how embarrassing. He's going to ask me to put something on.* She actually started looking around the room for something to throw over herself that would cover her. "What were you doing just now, when you were looking through the curtains?"

Mackenzie stared at him blankly. Is that all he wanted to know. She had to stop herself from grinning as she explained to him about the hot water system.

CHAPTER TWO

Introductions had been made soon after Mackenzie had gone over to have her shower. She wasn't sure if she should mention that she knew about him, at least knew about some of his background, although she had to admit that her information was somewhat sketchy. Jazz had provided her with some details but not enough to complete the whole picture.

Deciding in the end that discretion was the better part of valor, Mackenzie kept quiet about the little she knew about him. *If he wants to tell me anything about himself,* she reasoned, *he can do so himself.*

They were sitting in his kitchen, drinking coffee. The hot water system had been turned off; Mackenzie had showered and was dressed in a more appropriate fashion. She'd chosen a dark blue sundress, which showed off her natural colour. She conceded to herself that she just might make it back into the human race after all.

She was still not completely comfortable in this man's presence and had been making small talk in an effort to keep the silence at bay, but like dark storm clouds, it kept descending over them. She usually didn't have a problem holding up her end of a conversation, but this man was different somehow. She felt vulnerable around him, possibly due to the chain of events which had seemed to have come tumbling around her feet in a quick succession of disasters.

She had to admit to herself that she was just a little bit afraid of him, not in the physical sense, no, she didn't fear him in that way, but she was afraid of a brown-eyed stranger who brought out feelings in her that she found to be just the littlest bit disturbing.

Leaning forward in his chair to look at her intently, he asked casually, "Are you always this tense?" He'd been observing her as they'd been talking, noticing how straight she was sitting in her chair, and if she held her coffee cup any tighter, he was sure it was going to break.

"What?" Mackenzie knew she'd visibly started when the question had been fired at her.

Grinning at her obvious discomfort, he told her, "I wanted to know if you were always this tense. I've already told you that you're completely safe here with me, so the problem has to be with you."

"Problem?" Mackenzie looked at him, totally confused by his apparent line of reasoning. He seemed to be enjoying her total lack of composure. *Lord, he must think I'm a complete idiot. I can't seem to string two words together, let alone two sentences.* Mackenzie's stomach was tied up in knots as she tried to deal with her chaotic feelings regarding this man.

"In other words, loosen up. Talk to me, tell me about yourself. We'll start with something nice and easy, something safe . . . Um, let me see . . . okay, I've got it. Where do you work?"

Mackenzie was staring at him. What was happening here? What was he trying to do? She wasn't completely sure, but almost automatically, she found herself doing as she'd been bidden. He was a master of manipulation, and Mackenzie suspected that he was very aware of that particular fact. The words came out, haltingly at first, probably because she was still trying to fathom out the reason for his apparent interest in her.

"So you're a teacher," he said, raising his eyebrows. "Fancy that."

"Why should that be such a surprise to you?" She wanted to know a trifle indignantly. Didn't he credit her with enough brains to teach children? Although if she was to justify her erratic behaviour of the last few hours, she knew she would probably understand his natural skepticism.

"I'm a teacher," he told her matter-of-factly, looking at her intently in order to gauge her reaction.

"Fancy that," she threw at him in a mocking tone, borrowing his comment of a moment ago.

"Touché." He smiled across at her, and Mackenzie was treated to a burst of pure sunshine, which lit up his entire face. He continued, trying unsuccessfully to keep the laughter out of his voice, "Okay, enough of that."

"Oh, I see," she said, pushing her advantage while she could. "You can dish it out, but you don't like coping it in return, is that it?" She was unaware that her own features had taken on a lively exuberance which had put a bubbling sparkle into her eyes, a sparkle that had been absent for far too long.

"No, not really," he announced, still smiling.

"If you say so, but I just might reserve judgment on that one until I get to know you a little better," she told him before she realised what she'd said. *Oh no*, she thought, *I hope he doesn't think I meant anything sexual by that remark.* Her thoughts astounded her. In the three years since she'd been widowed, she hadn't particularly cared what people thought about remarks she'd made. Yet here she was, flying into an absolute panic over an innocent remark that she was sure he knew was made in jest. She quickly clutched onto the first thing to come into her mind, asking him where he was going to be teaching.

"Brendale High. Can you give me a rundown of the type of school it is? I've heard on the grapevine that it's got a bit of a reputation as being a tough place to teach, but then I always did like a challenge. It makes life just that little bit more interesting . . . What?" he asked as he saw the look on her face. She was looking at him through eyes that were wide with astonishment. Actually, she wasn't sure if the challenge he was speaking about was entirely aimed at the school. Perhaps he did think her comment of a moment ago had been sexual. Perhaps this was his way of letting her know that he was willing to be her partner in a sexual encounter. She could feel her skin starting to burn as she thought of him as a potential lover.

"Mackenzie?" he called her name, dragging her mind back to the present. He was looking at her, waiting for an answer to his spoken query.

"Oh, yes, um, sorry, I was just thinking of . . . Oh, never mind, it wasn't anything important," she told him as she tried to focus on their conversation. *Let me think*, she thought. He'd been asking about Brendale High, her school. "That's where I work. We aren't getting any new staff, that I know of, except for the new dep . . . Oh." She looked at him through fresh eyes. Dean Ashleigh was Rob's replacement.

Mackenzie experienced a momentary blast of anger directed at Rob for not telling her of the official status of her new neighbour. Admittedly, Jazz had told her he was a teacher, but nothing had been mentioned about his being the new deputy head at the school where she taught. That put a whole new slant on things. Sometimes fate could be so cruel. She could just imagine how their working relationship was going to proceed.

Oh well, she thought, tomorrow's another day. Maybe he'll have a change of heart. I'm good at what I do. Even he'll have to admit that fact when the time comes. Records don't lie. What good is crying going to do anyway? He already thinks you're a complete idiot, nothing can change that. Of all the people to move in next door.

Due to a curious chain of events, Mackenzie hadn't known who the new deputy head was going to be. She knew, of course, that Rob was being replaced. She'd even heard the new guy's name was Dean, but she'd been away with the flu when he'd been appointed, so she didn't know any details other than that. She'd been told by some of the females on staff that he was really something to look at, but more than that, he was supposed to be some sort of a mathematical genius. If this was the case, why was he giving up the teaching side of the classroom in favour of the administrative part of the school?

"Guilty as charged," he confirmed as Mackenzie continued to stare at him. "Judging by your reaction, I'm not exactly what you were expecting."

"No, um, I mean, yes, that is I . . . I didn't know who to expect," Mackenzie stammered truthfully, blushing furiously as she tried to regain her composure, which, for some obscure reason, had deserted her. She wondered how she'd cope with living next door to him and working with him during the day as well. She felt an unexpected sense of elation as her brain registered this fact. So why did she feel so edgy? Perhaps it was because she suspected a sharply inquisitive brain lurked behind that laid-back attitude he was projecting. What if he caught on to the fact that she found him attractive? It would be embarrassing. She wasn't sure it would be a good idea to work with this man, but then the decision wasn't hers to make. Anyway, it was a foregone conclusion, unless she was the one to leave. That idea wasn't as silly as it sounded because only the other day, she'd been offered another position in a country school. She hadn't entertained the idea at the time, but now perhaps she'd give it some further thought.

Shooting her another quick smile, Dean wanted to know, "Do you think you'll have a problem working with me?"

Considering the question before she answered, Mackenzie came to the conclusion that it wouldn't pose any problems that she wouldn't be able to handle. "No, I shouldn't think so, unless there's something you're not telling me." She was unable to stop the slight tremor that shook her slim frame as she looked across at him.

"Heaps, but we'll keep that for another time," he told her simply. If he noticed her unease, he chose to ignore it.

Their conversation after that became more general and centered on happenings concerned with the school. This pleased Mackenzie because she didn't want to talk about herself, and she instinctively knew that if she asked him questions of a personal nature, then she was leaving herself wide open for him to do the same with her. For some reason, she didn't want to tell him that she was a widow, not now; he might take it the wrong way, thinking she was throwing herself at him.

She stifled a yawn as she glanced around the room, looking for a clock. Her search was short lived as she spied a clock on the bench. It was a round, chrome timepiece decorated with ornate drawings which she couldn't clearly make out without drawing attention to the fact that she'd been pointedly looking at the time. The hands on the clock indicated that it was nearly two-thirty in the morning.

"Goodness, look at the time," she told him as she started to rise from her chair. "I'm sorry, I'm keeping you up. I had no idea it was

doing such a thing. His memory deserved better treatment than that from her.

The rest of Mackenzie's day was spent in utter dejection. Dean left as soon as he'd replaced the broken washer, which he seemed to fix in record time, but not before refusing, rather curtly, her invitation to stay for a cup of coffee. Mackenzie suspected it was her reference to her dead husband that had caused the drastic change to come over him.

If he'd accepted her invitation, she would have told him that she was a widow, that she'd been by herself for the past three years. She didn't know why she kept mentioning Steve; it just seemed natural for her to do so. He'd been a good part of her life; she didn't see why she should suddenly shove him aside now that he was no longer alive. Jazz was always telling her that she was using the memory of her dead husband as a buffer against becoming involved with any other man. Mackenzie didn't think this was the case. Her mind went back to the conversation she'd had with Dean earlier that morning. She supposed there was no logical reason for Steve's name to be mentioned. She hadn't made a conscious effort to bring him into the conversation; it had just happened.

Perhaps if she went next door and tried to explain, he might understand. It might even be a good idea to invite him over for dinner. After all the work he'd done for her, it was the least she could do as a way of saying thank you.

Having made this decision, Mackenzie felt a lot better. The ball would then be in his court, so to speak. She saw no reason why they couldn't be friends. If his earlier change of attitude towards her had been caused by her mentioning Steve, then she was willing to set the record straight; but she wasn't prepared to run after him, when her only crime had been to talk about Steve whom she'd dearly loved. He would always have a special place in her heart regardless of whether she ever remarried again or not. If she ever considered marriage again, the man she married would have to accept her on those terms.

A small smile of anticipation lit up her face as she pondered the consequences of her actions. Surely, there wasn't anything suggestive in the act of inviting a man to her home for a meal. How many times in the past three years had she done that? Well, not many if she was to be honest with herself, but the thought of preparing a meal for her new neighbour filled her with pleasure. Now she'd certainly have to go to the shops for supplies as her cupboards were practically empty.

Mackenzie made a quick visit to the bedroom, where she freshened up by dabbing some sweet smelling perfume onto her wrists and the pressure points of her neck. She breathed deeply, loving the smell that filled the room. She ran a brush through her brown curls, trying to re-establish some sense of order to the thick cascade of hair that tumbled down her back. She gave a quick thought to changing her clothes but decided against doing this. She was wearing faded blue denim shorts which were frayed along the hem line. Her top was a petite pink and white knitted garment. The straps of the top were thin shoestrings which meant that Mackenzie wasn't wearing a bra. She'd never been bothered by this fact before, but now she looked at herself in the mirror, wondering if, after all, she should change her top.

Then she reasoned it wouldn't do for him to get the wrong idea. She was, after all, only offering him a meal. Anyway, he'd seen her this morning in her nightie and last night in her underwear, so what was she worrying about? Never-the-less, a small pulse had started beating at the base of her neck, which she would have been loath to explain had she been asked to do so.

Right! All set, she told herself as she was about to head out of her bedroom door. A lone photograph of Steve caught her eye, and she stopped momentarily to study it. Her eyes suddenly filled with tears, which she quickly wiped away as fond, loving memories came back to swamp her with their vivid images. Was she sure she wanted to do this? She could be letting herself in for a lot of heartache. Steve's smiling face looked up at her from the frame. Mackenzie remembered taking this particular shot. He was exuberant after finally taking the plunge off the side of a bridge in a bungee jump, but she'd been too scared to try, too scared of getting hurt; and because of her fears, she'd not taken up the challenge. Steve was urging her to try, to let go of the rope that held her captive. Mackenzie felt that now; Steve was telling her to let go of the lifeline that tied her to him. He was telling her to try again, not to be afraid. She silently said her good-byes before heading for the bathroom to wash her face. She knew she could rid herself of all traces of tears, but not of the dear, sweet man who had caused them to fall in the first place, at least not yet.

Mackenzie stepped out onto the verandah just in time to see Dean driving off in the company of the brunette woman from yesterday. She was thankful that they didn't see her, for she was sure that her face must be registering some of the disappointment she was experiencing at the sight of seeing him in the company of another woman.

"This is ridiculous," she muttered to herself, "totally and utterly ridiculous. The man only moved in yesterday, for heaven's sake. Nobody falls for anyone that quickly." *No,* she thought, *you're just piqued because you were wrong. Why don't you admit it?* The personal admonishment fell on deaf ears as she tried to rid herself of the empty feeling which had settled in the region of her heart.

The fact that this woman was with him yesterday should have alerted you to the fact that he was in some kind of a relationship.

"Actually, you fool," she told herself, "it did, but you chose to ignore the signs, and now look where it's landed you."

"Hang on!" she said aloud as she tried valiantly to sort through all of the different emotions that were assailing her. "If he's involved with another woman, why did he get so upset this morning when I mentioned Steve?" Maybe it wasn't Steve's name that had set him off after all, but something entirely different altogether. Mackenzie was totally confused until a random thought struck her.

"Maybe he's the type of man who likes to have a string of girls in tow. Maybe he just wanted to add me to the list." Even as she voiced this explanation to herself, she had to admit that it didn't sound at all feasible; but she thought dejectedly that as an explanation, it would have to do until a better one presented itself.

The shrill ring of the telephone broke into her troubled thoughts. She smiled instantly as she recognised Jazz's voice. Once the pleasantries were over, she launched into a verbal attack. "Boy, are you lucky you're not here in person. I think I could literally strangle you without a second thought."

"Why, what's happened now?" Jazz wanted to know.

"As if you didn't know. Jazz, why didn't you tell me? Why did you let me find out from him?"

"Him, who?"

Mackenzie felt like screaming at her friend. "Jazz, this isn't the time for one of your silly jokes. You know who I mean, Dean Ashleigh. Why couldn't you have told me he was replacing Rob?"

"So you know already." Jazz confirmed. "How did you find out? You've obviously been talking. That's good."

"No, it's not, and you're evading my question, so help me, Jazz. Give me a straight answer, or I'll come down there and shake it out of you."

"I just thought it would give you something to talk about . . ."

"Something to talk about!" Mackenzie exploded, interrupting, "You've got to be kidding. Anyway, thanks to you, I'll probably be fired as an incompetent fool during his first week. I think I've made it to the top of his hit list already. The man totally hates me."

Mackenzie could hear Jazz chuckling into the phone. "Don't you laugh at me, Jazz Richards. I'm serious."

"Yes, I'm sure you are. Now calm down and tell me exactly what has got you so all fired up at this poor man after only one day."

Mackenzie haltingly told her about her midnight sojourn down into the front yard in an effort to fix the broken tap. Jazz was laughing so hard Mackenzie was tempted to hang up on her, but she knew her friend would badger her for the rest of the day if she didn't tell all.

"Oh, Mac, I wish I'd been there to see that sight. I can just imagine what the poor man must have been thinking when he saw you crawling around in the dirt, in your underwear no less." This brought a fresh attack of laughter from the other end of the phone as Jazz tried to come to terms with the story she'd just been told.

"It's obvious," she told Mackenzie, "that you like him. You're trying to hide it, but I think the lady doth protest too much."

"Rubbish," Mackenzie denied vehemently, "he's definitely not my type, so your little plan has failed."

"We'll see," Jazz's voice held a hint of victory as she thought of the woman on the other end of the line.

Her clear voice echoed around the classroom as twenty-five pairs of ears listened to her simple explanation of the task at hand. Everyone was looking at her, completely absorbed, until one of her students noticed that someone was standing in the open doorway.

"Graham, you'll learn more if you pay attention," she said to the errant student in question. This particular boy always had to be told to pay attention. His idea of the perfect day at school was to wag classes whenever he thought he could get away with it.

"But, Miss," the boy pointed out, "there's someone at the door." Mackenzie swung around, expecting to see a student with a message or another member of the staff. To her surprise, Dean Ashleigh stood there. She supposed that it had only been a matter of time before her teaching skills were put under the microscope. Feeling immediately angry with herself, she rescinded her catty thought of a moment ago. After all, the man was only trying to do his job. She'd have expected a visit from any other new member of the administrative staff, and she told herself contritely, *you would have made that person welcome in your classroom.* So what was she making a big deal about Dean for?

His unexpected appearance in her classroom unbalanced her. She'd been told by her fellow teachers that the new deputy head was doing the rounds of the classrooms in an effort to make himself familiar with the layout of the school. Mackenzie suspected it was also to check out for himself how the teaching staff handled themselves. *Well,* she thought indignantly, *he'd have to admit that when it came to teaching, I knew my way around the blackboard. Let him come in and watch me teach,* she fumed to herself. *See if I care.*

Schooling her expression to show not the slightest bit of emotion, she asked politely, "Yes, Mr. Ashleigh, what can I do for you?" She was pleased to note that her voice sounded normal and perfectly pitched, and her manner didn't show any of the uncertainty that was turning her stomach to a quivering mass of nerves at the very thought of coming face to face with this man, her would-be tormentor, not that he knew or even realised that Mackenzie viewed him in this light.

Dean explained his intentions before asking if he could have a few words with her students. He was the epitome of politeness as he smiled at her in a strictly businesslike manner. Not for a moment did his demeanor slip to reveal the other Dean Ashleigh, whom Mackenzie had come to know albeit only very briefly. She wondered if she'd ever see that particular side of his personality again.

Mackenzie nodded her agreement, saying politely, "Be my guest." She gestured with her arm, telling him that he could take over straight away. This gave her a perfect opportunity to study him. He had an easy going manner with the students, which she grudgingly had to admit she liked. She knew most of the students would respond to him, but she could also distinguish the strength in the timbre of his voice. She was under no illusions that her students would recognise that strength also. He was letting the students see that he was approachable but that he also demanded and expected total respect from them.

He asked if anyone had any questions to ask him and was amicable enough when it came to questions about his job, but he shied away from answering anything that broached onto his personal life. He'd perched himself on the side of her desk and seemed content to keep his back turned towards her the whole time, which suited Mackenzie just fine, or so she kept telling herself.

She liked the way he was dressed. He was wearing a sky blue shirt which suited his colouring. It was tailored to fit him, showing off his broad muscular chest and shoulders. His tie was a darker blue, which, for some reason, seemed to remind Mackenzie of his eyes. She knew this was ridiculous because his eyes were brown, like hers. Stealing covert glances at him, Mackenzie noticed that his slacks outlined his thighs because of the way he was sitting.

It's a good thing they aren't any tighter, she thought to herself, *or they'd be positively indecent.* Mackenzie was surprised by her line of thought, and she accidentally dropped the duster she'd been holding as her thoughts began to wander along inappropriate lines. The commotion briefly made her the centre of attention, and for a few seconds, every pair of eyes, including Dean's, turned in her direction to see what she'd done.

"Sorry," she told him as she looked into his eyes before bending down to once more gain possession of the offending piece of equipment. "I dropped the duster." She knew an explanation was unnecessary as everyone had come to that particular conclusion on their own. Looking in Dean's direction again, she was horrified to see that he was still looking at her.

Piercing brown eyes held her captive a moment longer than was necessary before he turned back to once more address the students. She'd been unable to read the message those brown orbs had been sending her, but she was sure he was inwardly laughing at her stupid behaviour.

When it seemed as if he was going to continue talking to the students well into the next lesson, Mackenzie had to interrupt, telling him that this particular lesson had now finished. It was time for this class to move on to their next classroom. He glanced at his watch, telling the students that Mrs. Phillips was correct; it was time to pack up and go to their next class. This information was met with a lot of negative feeling. Like all students, they jumped at the chance to have any unscheduled time away from lessons.

He briefly said his good-byes to the class but didn't leave the room. He smiled and stood aside, handing the class back to Mackenzie by gesturing in the same way that she'd done when she'd turned the class over to him. He gave her a look that was a trifle mocking, and Mackenzie instantly knew that the gesture had been intentional on his behalf. She smiled sweetly but said nothing. Instead, she gave out some homework before letting everyone leave. This caused a few grumbles of dissention, and some of the girls pleadingly tried to have Dean intercede on their behalf.

"No way," he told them jokingly. "Mrs. Phillips would eat me alive if I did that. Now go on, hurry up, and get to your next class."

Mackenzie noticed how many of the girls went out of their way to say good-bye to him. He gave them all a smile, telling them he'd see them later. *It was a nice smile*, Mackenzie thought. Open and friendly, similar to the ones she'd been treated to on Saturday night while they'd been drinking coffee. She found she missed that smile, and she wondered forlornly if she'd ever again be the sole recipient of one of his heart-warming smiles. She felt something akin to jealousy spread through her as she watched him talking to her students as they left the classroom, perhaps that was why she chose to ignore his next question to her. Thinking about it afterwards, she couldn't really say for sure what had prompted her to ignore him.

"You seem to run a good classroom," he told her when the last student was out of earshot.

She wasn't sure if he wanted an answer or not. He was probably just making an observation based on the little he'd seen, prior to his entering the room. Mackenzie chose not to answer, going instead to the blackboard where she started to wipe away the remnants of her lesson. This proved to be the wrong course of action on her part.

"Look," Dean ground out, taking a step closer to her than he really needed to, "I don't much like having to work with you either, but the least you can do is answer me when I'm talking to you." His voice was low and throbbed with suppressed emotion which was barely being kept under control. He continued, "If you're a professional and everyone around the place seems to think that you are, then at least have the courtesy to treat me as a professional also." Upon saying this, he spun round on his heel and began to walk away, leaving Mackenzie bereft and alone as she stood staring forlornly after him.

His verbal attack had hurt her, but with another class starting to assemble outside, now wasn't the time to ponder upon his reasons for attacking her as he had. She had to pull her emotions into gear as this particular year ten class had a tendency to be a little on the wild side if they weren't kept on a tight rein.

She allowed herself a glib retort, hoping it would help to soothe her frayed emotions. She mumbled to herself, "Now what brought that little tirade on?" Life had certainly become complicated since he'd walked into hers. Nobody in the class seemed to notice that their teacher was a little more subdued than was usually the case during the lesson, and for this, Mackenzie was truly thankful. After this lesson, Mackenzie had a spare period, which meant she could return to her staffroom and lick her wounds. She hoped that she'd have the staffroom to herself.

There was a note on her desk, telling her that there was a special morning tea in the teachers' common room to introduce everyone to the new deputy principal, Dean Ashleigh.

Oh no, Mackenzie thought wildly, *there's no way in hell that I'm going to turn up for that.* But she knew that if she didn't go, questions would be asked about her absence. She knew her feelings were still far too raw from the dressing down she'd unfairly received from him earlier.

The problem was solved for her when one of her friends marched petulantly into the staffroom and flung herself down at her desk.

"Sometimes life just isn't fair!" she stated to no one in particular.

"Why?" everyone with the exception of Mackenzie chorused.

"There's a morning tea for the new deputy principal, and I'm stuck with playground duty. I was looking forward to getting to know him better."

This outburst was met with several hoots of laughter, but no one offered to take her place. Mackenzie saw her friend's dilemma as her salvation.

"Bes, I'll do it for you," she offered lamely, hoping that no one would see through her scheme to get out of going. She added quickly as an afterthought, "I've met him, so it's not as if I have to be there. He came into one of my classes before."

"Oh, would you?" Bes crooned, smiling across at her. "I do Area 4 in the first half of the break."

Mackenzie nodded, only too glad to have a valid excuse not to attend. Area 4 was the playground; she couldn't get any further away from him if she'd sat down and planned it. *So why*, she asked herself, *do I suddenly feel like sitting down and crying?* She blamed her emotional state on delayed reaction stemming from Dean's verbal lashing earlier that morning.

The rest of Mackenzie's day was thankfully uneventful. She caught glimpses of Dean from a distance as he went about his business, but for the most part, he ignored her, which was what she wanted, was it not?

It was towards the end of the day when she was making her way to the photocopy room that Mackenzie ran into one of the administration staff.

"Mackenzie, good, I've been looking for you. Have you got a minute to spare?"

"For you, Jake, I'll find two or three," Mackenzie smiled at the man who stood before her. He was a short balding man to whom all of the office staff was pleasantly disposed. He possessed a jovial nature and was always ready with a quick smile or a cheerful joke for anyone he came into contact with.

"If I was just a few years younger young lady," he told her as he guided her towards Dean's office.

He had no idea of the nerves which had started to quiver unpleasantly in the pit of her stomach. Mackenzie started to feel physically ill as panic instantly fluttered through her again. She wasn't ready for another encounter with Dean. She was still smarting from their last meeting.

"Hang on, Jake, where are we going? I've got some work to do before my next class. I'm afraid I've been a bit lax today," Mackenzie told him as she realised where he was leading her. The last place she wanted to be was in the vicinity of Dean's office. She'd be quite surprised if he wanted to set eyes on her either.

Her assumption about Dean putting out the welcome mat for her had been correct, but to give him his due, he was polite, using his most reserved manner with her. She reasoned to herself that was probably due to the fact that there was another person in the room with them.

"Now, Dean, here's the young lady I was telling you about. Have you two been introduced properly yet?" He was smiling at them both as they eyed each other dubiously. Jake's smile was open and friendly as always. He continued before either of them could think of an appropriate response to his innocent inquiry, "I was looking for you at the morning tea, Mac. Where did you get to?"

Mackenzie launched into her explanation about how she'd swapped playground duty with Bes. She was saved from coming up with any more excuses when Jake interrupted her by saying, "What did I tell you, Dean. Isn't she something?"

"Yes, she's something alright," Dean agreed politely. Mackenzie threw him a pleading glance over the top of Jake's head. It was simply asking him not to make fun of this man. He was her friend. Dean briefly acknowledged her glance with an unperceivable nod of his head, but she still wasn't sure if he'd go along with her silent plea.

"Jake, you're making Mackenzie out to be a positive martyr." He grinned up at the older man, but Mackenzie knew that his words disguised his real feelings, where she was concerned.

"I hate to break this meeting up so soon," Mackenzie interrupted, "but I have a class in a few minutes, so if you two will excuse me, I really must go, or my students will start thinking they have a free period." Mackenzie tried to make her escape, but Dean's voice stopped her dead in her tracks, letting her know in no uncertain terms that she was going to stay.

"Hang on, Mackenzie, I really do need to talk to you." He smiled sweetly up at her as he reached for the phone. Mackenzie could see the determined effort he was making to be nice to her in front of the other man. She was under no illusions that she'd been foisted on him by Jake. The only thing was she hadn't the slightest idea why. Dean continued, talking into the phone, "Yes, Mary . . . Dean here . . . Yes, I'm fine." He chuckled as Mary said something that Mackenzie couldn't hear before adding, "I might take you up on that one day, but for now, I want you to take Mackenzie Phillip's class next period if you would. She's tied up at the moment and can't make it." Mackenzie stared at him. She couldn't believe he was doing this to her. Her eyes were like shards of ice as he casually looked up at her, asking her for details about her forthcoming lesson. And she thought furiously to herself, *he can flirt on his own time, not mine.*

"There," he said to her in a businesslike manner, "all done. Now you can sit down." He chose to ignore the icy look she'd thrown at him. Mackenzie had no choice but to comply with his wishes. Dean had effectively let her know, in no uncertain terms, that he was in charge of this particular situation, and the sooner she came to realise that fact, the better off she'd be.

She sat quietly, feeling like a caged animal. She still didn't know exactly why she'd been brought into his office. She looked up at Jake, hoping he'd be able to shed some light as to why she was here. Jake stood over her, looking like the cat that ate the preverbal bowl of cream. He obviously thought he'd delivered her into safe hands, but Mackenzie felt as if she was about to be devoured by Satan himself.

"Do you want to tell her, Dean, or shall I?" Jake looked across to Dean for confirmation. Mackenzie felt sure she wasn't going to like whatever it was she was about to hear.

"It's alright, Jake, I've kept you long enough." Dean stood up and walked around to the other side of his desk to formally usher Jake out of the room. He added as he placed a broad hand on the other man's shoulder, "I'll fill Mackenzie in on what she has to do."

"Just leave it to Mackenzie," Jake told him matter-of-factly. "She'll know what to do. Nothing fazes her. She'll sort you out in a jiffy, won't you, Mac?"

Mackenzie swallowed hard and managed a slight smile. She thought Dean was going to choke on the words he was trying so very hard not to say when he was told this last piece of information.

"I'm sure she will," was all he could manage to get out.

"Would you mind telling me what the hell is going on?" Mackenzie spat at him once Jake was out of earshot. She'd just about had enough of these silly mind games. Now was the time for answers, and she thought it was about time some of those answers were given to her.

Dean's manner was equally cold as he answered her impatient query. "If you attended staff meetings, you'd know what was going on."

Mackenzie stared at him blankly, having not the slightest idea what he was talking about. "There wasn't a staff meeting scheduled for today." She searched her brain, hoping that she hadn't forgotten. It wouldn't have been the first incompetent action she'd carried out in the few short days since he'd come into her life. Her brown eyes threw him a challenge. She knew she was right this time.

"There was a meeting called at morning tea. You were supposed to be there, but you were too busy with your Mother Teresa act to attend." He ground out the words, sounding as if his temper was about to snap completely.

She glared up at him, all pretense of niceness gone. "Just what's that supposed to mean?" That wayward lock of hair had fallen over his brow again, giving his countenance a less severe, almost boyish look, but Mackenzie was in no doubt that the man standing before her had long since left boyhood memories behind. The face that looked down into hers held suppressed anger, but there was a hint of something else there as well that was quickly veiled before Mackenzie could analyse it.

"Every time I speak to anyone around this place, the conversation eventually comes around to you. People are always singing your praises. It's like a bad dream that I can't wake up from." As soon as the words were out of his mouth, Dean knew he was in trouble. He hadn't meant to say them; now Mackenzie had another reason to dislike him. This was the last thing he'd wanted to happen. He was starting to wish he hadn't asked Jake to bring Mackenzie to his office. It was like she was two different people living in the same body. At their first meeting, he'd seen her as a brainless moron who was unable to string two words together coherently, and yet today she was being praised as Wonder Woman.

He tried to make amends by telling her, "Mackenzie, I'm sorry. I didn't mean that. Please forgive me." He could see his words were falling on deaf ears. His eyes searched her face, looking deeply into her eyes, trying to gauge if his apology had been accepted. She was sitting there, stony-faced, not showing emotion of any kind.

"There's nothing to forgive," she stated woodenly. "I like to help people, that's all." Mackenzie had gone numb. He'd as much as admitted that he disliked her. She couldn't remember ever being so hurt by anyone before. Her brain was whirling as she tried to think of an excuse, any excuse that would get her out of this room which had suddenly become very claustrophobic. Any excuse would do, but she knew she had to leave. She was very close to tears, but she resolved that she'd never let this man see just how much he was pulling at her already jangled emotions.

"Well, you wouldn't know it from where I'm sitting," he told her bluntly. He took a deep breath before he continued, "Look, Mackenzie, I don't want to fight with you. What say we call a truce to all of this bickering and make a fresh start?"

"I don't seem to have much of a choice, do I? If I say no, you'll use your position to pull me into line anyway, so I guess I'd better say yes and get it over and done with."

"Is that how you see me, as some sort of an ogre who uses his position to bully people into doing what they've been told?"

Mackenzie chose not to answer, letting her silence speak for her. Also, her throat was starting to constrict, and she wasn't sure that she was capable of answering without some of the emotion she was feeling breaking through. She steadfastly refused to look at him, choosing instead to focus her attention on a spot on the floor in front of her. She felt like a recalcitrant student who had been brought into the deputy's office and was refusing to respond to his suggestions to behave in a more amicable manner.

"Okay," he finally said when he realised he wasn't going to get any kind of a response out of her. He was staring unblinkingly at her as if weighing up everything that had happened between them in the confines of these four walls within the last forty minutes.

On hearing this, Mackenzie chanced a quick glance at him from under her long lashes. She could see a small pulse beating erratically at the base of his neck, which belied what he was really thinking. He was looking at her, so she looked quickly away again, only to find that her gaze was being inextricably drawn back to his face. *He had such a nice face*, she found herself thinking. It was full of angles and planes that she'd like to explore more fully if given the chance. She pulled her thoughts up sharply, knowing that if she continued down that particular avenue, she'd only get herself into trouble. It would be better to let him think that his jibes hadn't found fertile ground than to go around wearing her heart on her sleeve.

She summoned the last of her courage as she asked him, "Can I go now? It's been a long day, and I still have a few things to do before I leave." Her voice contained all of the pent up emotion she'd been trying so hard to keep buried.

"Yes . . . go," his answer was clipped, but Mackenzie didn't allow herself to reflect on the reason why. This was her chance to escape before he changed his mind. She literally flew out of her chair, across the room, to the door, and away to freedom without a backward glance, therefore missing the transformation that took place behind her. Instead of a man who had, only a few minutes before, been seethingly angry, there was now a man who looked very forlorn and deeply troubled.

In the weeks that followed, Mackenzie saw very little of Dean, both at school and as his neighbour. It was as if they had formed a silent pact to stay out of each other's way. If there was an instance where they found themselves in close proximity to each other, one of them would vacate the room whenever possible. Never would they occupy the same room if there was only the two of them present.

It was on one such occasion, when Mackenzie was in a hurry to pick up some papers from the front office, when she was sure Dean wasn't in the building. She was becoming adept at knowing his whereabouts in and out of the office. She thought if she was quick enough, she'd be gone before he made his return. She was starting to feel like a criminal who was on the run, always needing to know when it was safe to come out of hiding.

"Mackenzie, hi, we don't see you very much these days. Where have you been hiding yourself?" one of the office girls asked when she noticed who was coming through the door.

"Yes, I know," Mackenzie lied. "I have a couple of extra tutes that keep me on my toes these days. Some of the students are real little demons, you know the type."

The girl nodded in sympathy. "We have students up here all the time for Dean to speak to." It seemed the mere mention of Dean's name had the power to conjure him up out of nowhere.

"Is someone in here speaking my name in vain?" he joked as he poked his head around the adjoining door. He'd been making his way back to his office when he'd heard Sue saying something about him to the as-yet-unseen other person in the room.

It was only once he was in the room that Dean could see who Sue's visitor was. "Oh, hello, Mackenzie, I didn't see you there. How are you?" His face betrayed not an ounce of emotion as far as she could see. He could have been talking to a piece of wood. *Well, this is what you wanted*, she told herself. *He's doing you a favour, so stop sniveling. All of your bridges have been burnt with this man.*

Mackenzie had no choice but to answer him, but that didn't mean she had to stay in his vicinity; so after delivering a short response to his inquiry, she turned to Sue. "I can see that you're busy, so I'll call back later." Before Sue could respond in an affirmative or a negative way, she was gone, but she was conscious of Dean's eyes following her as she backed out of the door, making an awkward but hasty retreat.

"Mackenzie, hang on a minute, will you?" Dean's voice followed her as she made her way out of the now-empty classroom.

Turning around questioningly to look at him, Mackenzie waited until he'd caught up with her. Her initial reaction had been to keep walking, but she realised to do this would be childish and altogether stupid, no better than some of her students, in fact.

She schooled her features until she felt composed enough to face him. He'd quickly covered the distance between them, reminding her of an animal-of-prey advancing on its target. His body was long and lean, and he moved with complete confidence and co-ordination. She found she was watching him with something akin to fascination, until he came to a stop before her. She remained silent, letting him make the opening statement. He did, after all, call out to her.

"Thanks for waiting," he said casually, reminding her that she'd been thinking of running from him.

"Anytime," she told him as she looked him straight in the eyes. She was becoming a master at disguising her emotions where he was concerned, although this fact left her with a cold feeling in the pit of her stomach, feeling little joy in being his enemy, but she was given little choice in the matter.

"Damn it, Mackenzie, can't we have at least one conversation that isn't laced with sarcasm?" His look told her he was becoming exasperated with her childish antics regarding their relationship.

She opened her mouth ready with a retort, but seeing the defiant gleam in his eyes, she stood passively, waiting for him to resume the conversation. He never sought her out in this way, so presumably, he had something important to pass on to her.

The trouble was she didn't know if she could remain in his company without showing him some of the feelings she was harbouring towards him. Just being near him, hearing him speak in his deeply-timbered voice, was playing havoc with her nerves. She knew she had to concentrate on what he was saying; otherwise, her mind would start straying to other aspects of his manly physique.

"Are you listening to me?" he demanded of her as he stood towering over her.

"I'm sorry. Yes, I am. What was it you wanted to tell me?" Her manner changed, and she became more businesslike as she politely listened to him.

"Angie Webb has gone into premature labour." When he saw the look of concern that crossed her pale features, he hastened to assure her. "Don't worry, she's fine, but it means we're without an agricultural science teacher until a suitable replacement can be found. I've been told that on the odd occasion, you've stepped in and taken her classes."

Reluctantly, Mackenzie told him that she had, but it was an area that was outside of her own circle of expertise. She continued, "I guess I could do it, but how long is this expected to go on for?"

"Till the end of term," he told her, waiting for the explosion that he knew would follow this bit of information.

"But that's three weeks!" she wailed. "What am I going to do with them for three weeks?" Stepping in to do one lesson a month, when Angie had needed a pre-natal checkup, was one thing, but to take over completely, she wasn't sure she'd be able to give the students the help they needed in this particular area.

"Settle down and let me finish. I can help you, we can team teach if you think you can handle working with me." He was looking at her intently, trying to gauge her reaction to this bit of information.

"Team teach with you?" She was horrified, not being able to keep the disdainful look from clouding her face.

Dean threw her a look of pure malice, before telling her somewhat sternly, "Somehow I thought you might react in this way. Believe me, Mackenzie, if there was any other way around this, I'd gladly take it, but for now, it's the only option we have, so please try to be sensible, if not for my sake, then for Angie's."

Mackenzie knew he had her over a barrel. Besides, it wasn't the first time she'd taught in an area which was new to her. It wasn't so much that she'd be teaching this class that scared her but the fact that she'd be sharing the classroom with him. How was she going to mask her true feelings from him if they were forced into such close proximity? They'd have to plan lessons together which would mean more time spent in each other's company.

"Why can't a replacement be found who can start immediately?" Mackenzie wanted to know. She was frantically looking for a way out of this crazy situation, which had disaster written all over it.

"There wasn't anyone available in this particular field," he told her candidly, "so I thought if we were going to have someone teaching them who lacked experience, it was better to use one of our own teachers. At least the students know you, and what's more, they like you, so straight away that's a plus, wouldn't you say?"

Mackenzie found herself agreeing grudgingly, "I suppose so."

"Another thing that makes you a perfect candidate for the job is the fact that your timetable fits in perfectly. There won't have to be any rescheduling. I know it cuts down on your free time, giving you less time, etc., but it's only three lessons a week, one theory and a double practical. That's why I thought I could help, so surely, between the two of us, we can make it work."

"Why don't you just quit while you're ahead?" she warned, throwing him a rebellious look that spoke volumes about her present state of mind.

"You're probably right. I shouldn't try to oversell you on the subject, should I?" Mackenzie was sure she detected a small note of triumph in his voice, and she glanced up into his brown eyes, searching them for any signs of folly.

"Definitely not," came her quick retort. *What was the use of fighting him?* she thought calmly. *It will only create a fuss, and I'll probably still have to do it.* Just because he'd approached her about it didn't mean he was going to give her a choice. She was under no illusions that he'd made his mind up about this long before he'd approached her. "Anyway, I don't want Angie to worry, so I guess you can tell her that I'll give it a go . . . but I'm only doing it for her," she added quickly.

"I'll tell her," he said simply before tacking on as an afterthought, "I knew you wouldn't do it for me."

Mackenzie didn't know if he was poking fun at her or if he was being deadly serious. She scrutinised his face, looking for any signs which might give him away, but the look he was giving her was completely neutral, devoid of any feeling whatsoever.

"Look, can we get together later this afternoon?" He wanted to know, glancing at his watch. "I've got a meeting with an irate parent, and I don't want to be late."

"No, I can't. I've got a meeting of my own," she told him casually, not offering any more information on the subject.

"Fair enough, but we'll have to talk about it sooner or later," he told her directly. "Can you get in touch with me when you're ready to talk to me? But don't leave it too long."

Nodding her agreement, Mackenzie watched him as he walked away towards his office.

This week, she'd taken over Angie's classes, helped on and off by Dean who showed up whenever he had a spare minute. Mackenzie reluctantly admitted to herself that he knew what he was talking about when it came to explaining the processes involved with agriculture science. He had an easygoing manner with the students and seemed to be able to draw them easily into a conversation regarding any aspect of the lesson.

Today's lesson had left Mackenzie feeling bad tempered and slightly frazzled, a point that was quickly noticed by the students who told her that they didn't understand why she seemed to be picking on them for no apparent reason. She'd actually given out three detentions during the lesson for behaviour that really didn't warrant anything more than a reprimand. She'd been asked a simple question and had been forced to admit to the year twelve student that she wasn't sure of the answer. Dean had stepped in answering the boy's question to his obvious satisfaction because after that, most of the questions were directed towards him.

Mackenzie threw Dean a look which reeked of "I told you so" before her attention was claimed by another student who needed some help. She gratefully pulled up a chair, sitting beside the girl, hoping that together, they could find a solution to the question before them. By the end of the lesson, they were no closer to finding an answer that satisfied either one of them.

This is ridiculous, fumed Mackenzie. Never before had she felt so incompetent in the classroom. She was determined that one way or another, this ridiculous situation was going to end. As soon as the last student had filed out of the classroom and was safely out of earshot, she rounded on Dean, lashing out at him, venting her pent up anger on him as if he was her personal whipping boy. "Damn it, Dean, didn't I tell you this wouldn't work?"

"It went okay," he told her casually, totally ignoring the mortified look on her face. He was erasing diagrams from the blackboard, and it seemed to Mackenzie that he wasn't paying the slightest bit of attention to the point she was trying to make.

"You don't need me in this classroom. The only reason that I can think of for your wanting me here is to humiliate me in front of my students," Mackenzie told him. She knew she was probably clutching at straws, but she just couldn't think of another feasible reason for his wanting her to be in the classroom when he was so competent himself. Was he letting her know in his own way that he was in charge, and she had to toe the line or suffer the circumstances?

"Is that so?" Dean claimed as he turned around to face her. He was leaning against the whiteboard and had folded his arms loosely across his broad, masculine chest, giving Mackenzie the false impression that he was perfectly at ease, but underneath his calm exterior, he felt like a coiled spring, ready to unleash its power.

He stared at her for a few seconds before he asked, "Now where in the world did that accusation come from. Do you know you're the most irritating woman I've ever met? You see problems where there are none. Would you mind explaining to this mere male where you pulled that notion from? Because I'd be very interested in hearing about the different ways in which I have humiliated you."

Mackenzie licked her lips which had suddenly gone very dry. "Perhaps humiliate was the wrong word," she hedged, knowing that she'd once again overstepped the mark where Dean was concerned. Why did she always have to act like a complete idiot in his presence? She already knew the answer to that particular scenario. She did it for self-preservation, to protect herself against his particular brand of charm because if she didn't, she was in danger of falling in way over her head. It was better to erect this barrier now to be safe.

"Perhaps," Dean agreed as he pushed himself away from the blackboard using his broad shoulder as leverage.

His sudden movement towards her caused Mackenzie to retreat hastily backwards. This was a move which proved to be disastrous because she made contact with a chair which had not been properly pushed under a desk. She would have fallen had it not been for Dean's quick action to steady her.

"See what happens when you try to run away?" he told her glibly as he held her in a casual embrace from which she could have pulled free at any time.

Every nerve ending in Mackenzie's body had started to vibrate from Dean's random touch. It was all she could do to nonchalantly stand passively in front of him without flinching away from his strong arms like a frightened kitten.

Taking a deep breath to steady herself, she told him, "I'll bear it in mind next time I'm being . . . um, helped." She finished lamely, looking up into his long angular face. He lifted his eyebrows and was staring at her, probably expecting another jibe. She ruefully thought of all the other times during their short acquaintance when she'd used her powers of female reasoning to help her out of similar situations with him. Was it any wonder then that he was looking at her now expecting the worst?

"See that you do. You might be pleasantly surprised by the outcome," he said as he headed for the door.

Mackenzie wasn't sure why she tagged along, but she found herself walking beside him as he made his way towards the administration block.

"Was ag science one of your teaching areas, or have you just picked it up along the way?" she asked casually, more for something to say than for any burning desire to know the answer. He could have told her about the man in the moon, and she would have listened with rapt attention. Her skin was still tingling from the casual contact he'd endowed upon her a few minutes ago in the classroom.

He must have been surprised by her obvious interest into his background because he gave her a skeptical look which spoke volumes without him having to say a word.

"What?" Mackenzie asked as she looked up at him. "Can't I ask a simple question about your particular teaching areas, or is that subject taboo?"

"Sure you can, but given our track record, it's just unusual for you to want to speak to me at all. You've just thrown me a little, that's all." He frowned slightly as he looked down at her. A lock of hair had fallen down over his forehead, and he subconsciously brushed it away with the back of his hand.

"Maybe I'm trying to atone for my earlier behaviour,"

"Which part?" he interjected lightly, trying not to smile as he looked at her.

"A girl can change her mind you know." Mackenzie wasn't sure what was happening. She only knew that she felt light-hearted and happy for the first time in weeks. *It's marvelous what a casual caress can do*, she thought idly. *I wonder how I'd respond to a more serious encounter, one that involved more than an accidental touch.*

Mackenzie was treated to a heart-warming smile which started her pulses hammering in her veins. She knew this smile, and her heart responded to it automatically.

"It seems they can at that," Dean answered, responding to her apparent change of mood. His smile reached his eyes, making them look like twin orbs of shimmering chocolate pools.

"So?" she challenged, still waiting for an answer.

"So what?" Dean wanted to know, puzzled by her question until it dawned on him that he hadn't answered her earlier enquiry.

"Oh, yes . . . right . . . the ag science. Well, let me see. I guess most of my knowledge comes from the three years I spent at Clermont High, when I did my country service. I used to go out to one of the local property's whenever I had the chance. I guess some of the country rubbed off on me."

"Do you miss it, the country I mean?"

"Sometimes. It was a good life. The people were great. They worked hard, played hard too."

They'd reached the foot of the administration steps when Sue, one of the office girls, poked her head around the corner of the building.

"Ah, just the two people I've been looking for. You both have people looking for you." At the look of inquiry that she got from both of them, she continued, looking first at Mackenzie before saying, "Steve wants you to phone him, Mac, ASAP, and Dean,

Meredyth is waiting for you in your office. She said to tell you she's
lost her key to your place, so she can't get in. It sounds like she's in
a bit of a pickle, groceries melting all over the place and all that."

Mackenzie was overjoyed at her piece of news. It had been three
months since she'd seen her brother. "Great, it's about time he came
to see me," she said enthusiastically, trying to ignore the sharp pang
she felt at hearing the news that Dean also had a visitor waiting
for him. Well, it only confirmed her worst fears; Dean did have
someone. Meredyth was probably the woman who was with him on
that first day when he'd called in for the house key.

"That sounds about normal for her," Dean told Sue. "She's
always losing something."

He turned to look at Mackenzie, but his joyful outlook of a few
moments ago had been replaced with a more somber expression.
"I'll have to get back to you about those lessons. Perhaps it would
be better if someone else could do them after all." Upon saying this,
he turned and vaulted up the stairs, leaving Mackenzie standing,
staring after him. She knew he was right about the lessons, so
why did she feel so desolate? It seemed that her good humour of a
few minutes ago had also vanished, leaving her feeling empty and
alone.

A few days later, as Mackenzie was walking towards her car, she
was stopped by one of her friends who wanted to know if she was
joining them for a drink to herald in the start of the weekend.

"No can do," she said happily. "Steve's due in today for a brief
stopover. I'm not sure what he'll want to do." Mackenzie looked
forward to these meetings with her brother. They were few and far
between, due mainly to his busy work schedule as an airline pilot.
The fact that her husband's name had also been Steve had always
been a sweet coincidence to her.

"Righto. Say hello from all of us. How long has it been since you've seen him this time?"

"About three months," Mackenzie answered simply as she eased herself into her car, catching sight of Dean walking to his own vehicle as she did so. His face was set, and if Mackenzie was any judge of body language, he looked to be blazingly angry about something. She wondered what had happened to make his face look so thunderous and dark.

She wished she could go over to him to ask what was wrong, but that was impossible. She'd have liked to be able to soothe the frown away from his handsome brow, but it wasn't her place to do so. Anyway, what could she possibly say to him that would make a difference? He definitely didn't look to be in a mood that would generate any sort of warm feeling between the two of them. The barriers between them were back up and firmly in place. It was as if their carefree conversation of the other day had been wiped away. *No,* she thought sadly, *he was better left alone. Besides, there was always Meredyth. Let her soothe the savage beast.* The thought of the brunette woman put a damper on Mackenzie's happy mood of a few minutes ago, but she resolved to push them both out of her mind. She didn't want to meet Steve with anything troublesome on her mind, but she couldn't control the flighty feeling from settling in the pit of her stomach at the very sight of Dean.

Mackenzie only had time to take a quick shower, throw on some fresh clothes, and then it was time to meet Steve. She was sure he could find a more suitable companion with whom he could spend his precious off-duty hours, but she was always assured that he saved this particular port of call especially for her.

They spent the next few hours together, with Steve telling her about the various places he'd visited since their last meeting. He had an assortment of knick-knacks for her, which he told her could be added to her growing collection of totally useless objects, adding that fairly soon, she'd have something from just about every corner of the earth.

Being with Steve meant that for a little while at least, she could forget about the trauma that was taking place in her own life. He had her laughing about some of the antics of the elderly passengers who chose to fly with his airline.

"Honestly," he told her, "you'd think that if they were so freaked out by flying, they'd go by train or bus or boat, but no . . . they have to make my life miserable and choose to have their hysterics thirty-five thousand feet in the air."

Mackenzie had spent a particularly trying week. She'd be glad when she could officially call it a day. For the last two hours, she'd been closeted up with the school counselor, Mark Ferris. One of her year twelve students, a raucous boy at the best of times, had filed a complaint about her which stated that she'd deliberately placed her hand on his thigh in a suggestive manner. The boy would not rescind his allegation and complaints of this nature had to be taken seriously to protect both parties.

"Mark, it's simply not true," Mackenzie said again. "I don't know why he's done this but I . . ." Tears filled her eyes, and she tried valiantly to stop them from falling.

"Mackenzie, you know I have to go through the motions. I don't believe you did either, but the kid has made a complaint which has to be investigated. Can you remember if you touched him at all?" At Mackenzie's mortified look, he rephrased the question, "I mean, have you ever patted him on the shoulder? Has there ever been any body contact between you at all?"

Mackenzie wiped her eyes with the back of her hand. She didn't need to think before answering the proposed question. She explained, "Yes, but only as a gesture of encouragement and then only on the shoulder. It's something that I've always done with boys and girls alike. I've certainly never tried to come on to any of my male students. It's ridiculous. I'm being set up, but I have no idea why he'd want to do it."

"We'll get to the bottom of this, don't worry. Given Brad's record, I'm sure we'll find it's a hoax of some sort. We're trying to get in touch with his parents, maybe they can shed some light on things."

Mark's reassurances didn't mean very much to Mackenzie at the moment. If she was found guilty, she could lose her job, not to mention the respect of the teaching community at large. When things like this had happened to other teachers in the past, whether they'd been guilty or innocent, a little bit of mud had always stuck to the innocent party, tarnishing an unblemished record for all time because there would always be an element of doubt in people's minds.

There was a brief knock at Mark's door, and then to Mackenzie's consternation, Dean stood in the doorway. His face was a closed book, so Mackenzie didn't know what to expect from him. He entered the room and closed the door, so obviously, he didn't want anyone outside of these four walls to hear the words he was going to say to her. The nerves in her stomach tightened as she forced herself to look up at him. For some reason that she still couldn't define, she needed Dean to believe in her innocence. She realised that his trust meant a lot to her, but she was the last person he'd give his trust to. This would be the chance he'd been looking for, to finally see the back of her. She watched with a sinking heart as he pulled a piece of paper from his shirt pocket. She was sure he was going to give her her walking orders.

Instead, he faced her squarely, telling her bluntly, "The boy remains adamant." Dean held the flimsy piece of coloured paper in his hand as his eyes quickly scanned the contents yet again. "He's not going to change his mind. Is there anything else you want to add?" His clear brown eyes scanned her face intently as if he was searching for his own clues to this investigation. She didn't pull back or look away but let him scour her face with his eyes. She knew she had nothing to hide.

"No, there's nothing else," Mackenzie answered him in a firm, clear voice. He'd never know the effort it cost her to sound as calm as she did. Her answer was final as she focused her brown gaze onto his own piercing brown eyes which still held hers. She'd been clenching her fists, ready for a fight, but now she simply let her hands fall limply into her lap. *What's the use?* she told herself forlornly, growing tired of the continued animosity that she'd helped to build between them.

Dean noticed her body language deteriorate from being quietly confident as it had been since this god awful mess had started to slowly take on the worried frown she was trying so valiantly to hide from everyone. He was under no illusions that he topped her list of people that she didn't want to see her crumble. He wanted to hold her, to soothe away the troubled lines he saw settling on her forehead. He wanted to kiss everything away to make things better for her, but he knew he'd be pushed away. He was the last person she'd accept help from. He hoped Steve was there for her. It made him feel slightly happier to know that she had someone to lean on in times of trouble. He ignored the tight feeling he always got in the pit of his stomach every time he thought of Mackenzie being with Steve, even though he knew he had absolutely no right to have an opinion on this subject in any way, shape, or form.

Dean was preparing to leave, having found out from Mackenzie what he already knew to be the truth. He had his hand on the doorknob, when out of the blue, he turned abruptly and simply said, "I know I'm not supposed to take sides, but for what it's worth, I believe you, Mackenzie. We'll get to the bottom of this. Don't worry, okay?"

"Don't!" Mackenzie flung at him angrily, trying to keep her voice even. "Don't patronize me now. I don't want your pity." Her nerves were ready to snap.

"Then what do you want from me?" he asked, coming back into the room to stand in front of her. His voice was low and clipped while his eyes glittered coldly under dark brows. Upon delivering this abrupt statement, he turned sharply on his heel and quickly left the room.

His outburst took Mackenzie completely by surprise. It was the last straw as far as she was concerned. Being told by Dean that he believed in her was positive news. She hadn't expected to hear encouragement of this nature from him. The tears that she'd been trying to keep at bay for so long now ran freely down her face. She put her head into her hands and wept, needing to release the pent up emotions which had been steadily building up within her.

CHAPTER THREE

"I think we could all do with a drink!" This was the general consensus of the whole staffroom when Mackenzie finally reached her desk at the end of the day to gather up her belongings.

"What do you say, Mackenzie? It will be our shout," her friends were telling her in their own way, exactly what they thought of the charges she was facing.

The news of her supposed flirtatious adventure had filtered down through the staff grapevine, and her fellow teachers had been letting her know in no uncertain terms that she could count on their support. Some hugged her, saying they were shocked by the boy's attempt at putting something like this onto her in this manner.

Mackenzie's initial reaction had been to say no. She felt like running away and hiding, but she knew she was going home to an empty house where she'd probably spend the coming week-end worrying and moping over her problems. Her thoughts must have shown on her face because everyone started to make their way over to where she sat perched on the top of her desk.

"We won't take no for an answer this time. For the last few weeks, you've been dodging everyone. You've said no to every invitation we've thrown your way," Brian told her. Everyone nodded their heads in agreement before he added sadly, "We'll start to think you don't like us anymore."

Cherry, a petite, young woman, piped in, "Have you got a man tucked away somewhere? Someone you don't want to share with the rest of us females?"

Mackenzie laughed, telling her nothing could be further from the truth. "Alright, I'll come, but only for a little while," she agreed at last. Actually, spending some time with her friends would be a good morale booster. Maybe she'd be able to relax and share some pleasant company. She'd been spending way too much time on her own lately, closeted up in her house, afraid to step outside in case she ran into Dean Ashleigh.

The only good thing her forced hibernation had done for her was that now, she was completely up to date with all of her work. She'd even written up two new units of work for her year nine English class and had started on a third. She reflected grimly to herself that it was time she gave up acting so childishly and began to act in a more responsible manner. It was time she accepted the fact that Dean Ashleigh wasn't attracted to her and get on with her life.

A short time later found them all seated around a giant table, which they had made by pushing together some of the smaller tables. The bar staff was used to them doing this, so not an eyebrow was raised in their direction. This was one group who were good customers. They came in and had a few drinks, usually on a Friday afternoon; they were orderly and kept their noise level down to a dull roar, which was more than could be said for a lot of the patrons who drank here.

Mackenzie tried to get her purse out of her bag, but she was promptly told to put her money away. "It's our shout, remember, Mac? Are you going to have your usual?"

Reluctantly, Mackenzie smiled at the group of people sitting around the table before saying, "I'm not sure I should let you do this, but yes, I'll have my usual. Thank you, all of you, for believing in me." Her eyes misted over as she tried to find some appropriate words that would let everyone know how she was feeling towards all of them at this particular moment.

"Here, drink this," someone thrust a frosted glass of scotch and ginger ale into her hand, which she gratefully accepted. Anything was better than blubbering over everyone as she was in danger of doing.

She skulled the drink, only realising afterwards, when she put the empty glass back onto the table, that it had been way stronger than she was used to drinking.

"Woo-ooh . . . way to go, Mac. We'll make a drinker out of you yet," one of the immediate group told her laughingly, slapping her on the back.

Mackenzie felt the alcohol immediately starting to permeate through her unresisting blood stream. She knew she'd have to slow down, or she wouldn't be able to stand up, let alone drive home. Not only that, she'd have a giant hangover to contend with in the morning.

"Please," she said to her fellow drinkers as they sat, talking about anything and everything, "the drinks are way too strong. I'm going to end up pie-eyed if I keep this up." Already, there was another drink waiting in front of her. She knew it would be in her best interests to let it sit there for a little while longer.

"Rubbish. Mackenzie, it's time you started to enjoy yourself again. You've been way too serious lately," Brian told her. He'd always taken a fatherly attitude with the younger members of the staff.

"Hey, here comes Dean . . . Hey, Dean, over here," someone in the group called out. The invitation was chorused by everyone at the table, with the exception of Mackenzie, but none seemed to notice her lack of friendliness towards Dean Ashleigh.

He certainly was a magnificent specimen, Mackenzie found herself thinking. His long, lean body moved like a well-cared-for machine. He smiled as he saw everyone and changed his direction, covering the distance in just a few short strides. On closer inspection, Mackenzie could see several grooves of tiredness etched into the fine lines around his eyes. She surprised herself when her befuddled brain told her it would be nice to be the one who got to kiss those lines away from his face. He'd removed his tie and unbuttoned the top of his shirt, revealing a heavy matte of hair, which Mackenzie had found fascinating the very first time she'd seen it. Now she'd like nothing better than to run her fingers through that manly mane.

The scotch Mackenzie had been consuming at a steady pace was starting to numb her brain. After a few hours, she was having trouble concentrating on the conversation, and she was starting to feel slightly dizzy. Under any other circumstances, she would have heeded the warning signs which her body was sending her, but she thought dazedly, *These are not ordinary circumstances. How many times in your life do you face two dilemmas at the same time? Some stupid kid puts you in a compromising position which could end up costing you your job, never mind that you're innocent, then there was the age-old story of unrequited love*, and she seemed to have a bad case of the latter. Had she been thinking clearly, Mackenzie would have realised what she was finally admitting to herself. Her animosity towards this man covered something that went a lot deeper. She loved Dean Ashleigh.

"What are you lot of alcos doing here?" he joked, looking around the table. "You've certainly made an early start of it today, haven't you?" Suddenly his gaze fell on Mackenzie, and his smile flickered for a fraction of a second before becoming fixed and rigid as he looked at her, taking note of her inebriated condition. She looked back at him through eyes which weren't completely focused.

"Have you come here to join us?" Brian wanted to know. He'd already begun to reorganise people around the table so that Dean could sit down.

Mackenzie's head was beginning to spin like a whirling dervish, and she knew she'd definitely reached her cut-off point.

"Okay, if you insist," Dean answered casually. He'd actually been on his way to the bottle department where he was going to buy the biggest bottle of rum he could find to help him drown his sorrows. He'd just come out of a grueling three-hour meeting with the parents of the kid who had made the allegations against Mackenzie. He felt frustrated and angry because he hadn't been able to make any headway in proclaiming her innocence. It had turned into a heated debate, with insults being hurled at him and the school. It was in times such as this that Dean wondered why he'd chosen to go into teaching at all. He'd finally had to call a halt to the proceedings, afraid he'd lose his temper completely with the argumentative couple who sat before him. He was only too happy to join the crowd of happy drinkers. Maybe some of their jovial spirits would rub off on to him. He certainly could use some happy thoughts right about now.

"Are you celebrating anything special, or is this just a normal Friday night fling?" he asked as he took the chair which was being offered to him.

"Are we ever," Brian pointed to where Mackenzie was sitting. "We're here to cheer Mackenzie up. Aren't we, Mac? She's been going through a rough time lately. You wouldn't know, only being here a month or so yourself, but she just hasn't been herself lately."

Everyone in the group chorused Brian's sentiments. Once started down this particular road, Brian could get very boring. Mackenzie could feel her spirits falling. She wasn't in the mood to have her miserable life story trotted out yet again for everyone to hear. Besides, it was old news. The last thing she wanted to hear at this moment was the dragged-out version of her life in vibrant living colour. She could just picture Dean's reaction to her marital status. Poor little Mackenzie, widowed and alone. She wasn't going to be humiliated in front of him. He could find out at some other time, when she wasn't around to see the derision in his eyes.

"Brian, please don't bore him with stories about me," Mackenzie pleaded, when it looked as if Brian was about to launch into the story of her life. The last thing she needed, or wanted, was to be reminded of Steve. Was it any wonder she was having a hard time forgetting him, when everyone around her kept bringing him up?

Brian had turned to look at her, smilingly, letting her know that he only had her best interests at heart. "Do you know what you need, Mac?" he started to say. "You need . . ."

Oh no, here it comes, Mackenzie thought frantically. Brian was about to launch into his pet project about finding a man to look after her. That was the last thing she needed to hear. How humiliating would it be to have Dean Ashleigh hear how everyone in the school wanted to find her a man. It would sound like she was incapable of attracting a member of the opposite sex for herself. What a laugh he'd get out of that one. There was no way Mackenzie was going to let this conversation run its course.

She interrupted Brian, saying the first thing that came into her head, "Do you know what your problem is, Brian? You've been teaching English literature for way too long." She knew her remark sounded out of place, but it seemed to have the desired effect. Brian stopped talking and looked across at her, totally confused.

"How so?" he wanted to know.

All eyes around the table were now fixed on her, making her the centre of attention as everyone waited for a coherent explanation to her seemingly unrelated outburst. She chanced a quick look across at Dean and found he was looking at her somewhat skeptically. His look was telling her, in no uncertain terms, that he was aware of what she'd just done. What he couldn't fathom was why. She stared back defiantly, her courage boosted, no doubt, from the large number of drinks she'd consumed. A small smile formed on her lips, but it soon faded as she saw his eyes go cold as he stared at her. It had been a hollow victory, after all.

Someone had put another drink down in front of her, and she drank it, uncaring at the moment of the consequences which were sure to follow tomorrow, when she'd have a banger of a hangover.

"Um . . . well, I mean, you see everything as if it were part of a novel. There aren't always happy endings, you know. Look at Shakespeare, for instance, Romeo and Juliet. Now there was a tragedy." Mackenzie had hit on one of Brian's favourite subjects, and soon, he was off on another tirade about misbegotten love, but this time, thankfully, it didn't concern her and for that, she was thankful.

The rest of the group had started to groan. They knew once Brian started on this subject, especially with a few drinks under his belt, that he was unstoppable.

Music had started up in the background. Mackenzie thought it was only fair since she'd started him off; she should be the one to cart Brian off onto the dance floor. She was fairly certain no other member of the group would start up the conversation again. She rose unsteadily to her feet and slowly made her way around the table, meaning to grab Brian. She thought if she could get him onto the dance floor, he could tell her in private about her flagging love life. Then by the time they sat down, her lecture from him would be over, and she'd be out of danger.

"Come on, Brian," she said as she grabbed him by the collar. "Come and dance with me, and stop boring these nice people to death." There were grunts of ascension from around the table. She wasn't quite game to look in Dean's direction, for she knew his brown eyes would probably be laughing at her childish antics.

"I think if I got up to dance, I'd fall flat on my face, Mac," Brian told her apologetically, then added as he had a bright idea, "I'm sure Dean would love to dance with you, wouldn't you, Dean? Besides, he's probably the only one here sober enough to take you on."

Mackenzie felt trapped. She had nowhere to run. She was sure Dean would say no anyway, but to her surprise, he said, "Sure, why not?"

"No, no, it's alright, really, I just didn't want this old codger bothering everyone with a very boring, very old story, that's all," Mackenzie stammered. Her head was spinning, and she was sure it wasn't only from the drinks she'd consumed over the course of the evening.

"Nonsense, you get out there and have that dance," Brian pushed her towards Dean who had come to stand by her side. She found she had to literally hold onto him to keep from falling.

"Sorry," she mumbled halfheartedly as she pushed herself away from him. She wasn't exactly sure why she was apologising. Was it because she'd fallen into him, or because he was being forced to dance with her?

She looked up at him, noticing a slight smirk had covered his handsome features. She couldn't understand what was so funny. It wasn't fair that he was laughing at her.

To make matters worse, the music had changed from the fast and lively rock and roll song of a few minutes ago to a soft dreamy number that cried out for lovers to come and express themselves in each other's arms. Mackenzie didn't know what to do. She stood, looking at Dean uncertainly. She'd take her lead from him.

"Come on," he teased when he saw the horrified look she was sending him. "You can't have everything your own way. I promise I won't bite."

Mackenzie was baffled by his comment, but she could see she had no choice but to do as she'd been bidden. She looked back towards the table, hoping she could perhaps stage an escape, but everyone was in deep conversation. They weren't taking the slightest bit of notice of the couple who now stood on the edge of the dance floor.

Dean noticed her fleeting look towards their table and told her smugly, "No help from there, I'm afraid. It looks like you're stuck with me for the duration."

She couldn't understand why he was humiliating her like this. Was he deriving some sort of sick pleasure from seeing her in distress? She didn't know why, but she had to take a shot at him. Probably because she was scared he'd guess that she really wanted, very badly, to be held in his strong arms. To be enfolded close to him, to feel his every move through her own body.

She glared up at him, saying waspishly in a soft undertone, "I'm only doing this because I have to." She knew it was nasty and instantly wished she could take the horrible words back, but it was too late. The damage had been done. She saw the slight frown contort his handsome features before he shrugged and once again smiled at her, almost as if he'd guessed the reason why she'd said those hurtful words.

"If you say so. Come on, let's get this over with," he told her as he led her further onto the dance floor.

Mackenzie was glad that they weren't the only couple who had opted to dance to this particular bracket of songs. It meant that they could blend in, becoming invisible. She knew it would be apparent to anyone who cared to look at them that they weren't close. Their body language wasn't compatible.

At first, they moved around the dance floor like complete strangers, standing apart, not touching. Mackenzie could never be sure afterwards which one of them had bridged the ominous gap that had been keeping them apart, but suddenly, she found they were moving together as one to the soft beat of the music. Dean's hands were now linked casually around her waist, while her own hands had somehow found their way to his muscular chest and were now resting softly against the strength of him. She was wondering if she should push herself away from him, when the problem was taken out of her hands completely. He took hold of her hands and casually placed them up and around his neck, giving her no choice but to hold onto him. He then put his own hands back where they'd been before. He looked down, telling her matter-of-factly, "It's more comfortable this way."

"Oh," was all she could think of to say to him as they resumed their slow movement around the dance floor.

Don't get so flustered, she chided herself silently. *He's only a man, he's only a man, he's only a man*, she chanted to herself. Yes, but what a man her heart cried as he held her loosely in his arms.

She wanted so badly to give herself up to this magical moment, to give her heightened senses the satisfaction they were wildly crying out for. She wanted to be able to feel him against her. She concluded that if she moved in just a little bit closer, she could have her heart's desire. *He probably won't notice anyway,* she thought. *He's probably not even thinking about us. He's probably thinking about work or what he can have for dinner when he gets home.*

She brazenly moved in closer to him. Her body immediately responded to his closeness. She felt content, but her happiness was short lived as he moved slightly away from her. She was forced to look up at him, feeling humiliated and embarrassed.

One dark eyebrow lifted questioningly as he asked casually, "Does this mean the war is over, or do we just have a temporary truce?"

Mackenzie tried to pull further away from him, furious with herself that she could let her guard down with this man so easily, but her efforts were thwarted, and she was instantly pulled back into his firm embrace. She couldn't let herself relax; she was scared. Her body was sending out traitorous signals that she was finding very hard to control. She decided it was far better for her to stay alert. She wasn't going to answer his obvious attempt to taunt her.

They continued to dance in this manner for a few minutes more before Dean whispered into her ear, "Loosen up, you feel as stiff as a board."

Mackenzie could remember having sweet nothings whispered into her ear on past occasions, but never had she been asked something as bizarre as this request. His words had the desired effect. It was as if all of her animosity towards him melted away, leaving in its place a hole which could be filled with something more tangible and real.

She felt herself starting to chuckle in spite of herself. Looking up at him, she saw eyes that held a glint of mischief in their depths.

"That's better," he said as he held her closer to him. "I like this much better." He liked the way she seemed to fit exactly against him.

Their bodies were finally moving as one complete unit. Mackenzie could feel the hard length of him as he held her securely. His strong arms held her in his masculine embrace. She felt at home here in his arms. She knew she was courting trouble, for as soon as they left the dance floor, she was under no illusions that she'd be right back to avoiding him, probably even more so than before.

He was just being kind, she surmised, and she was being a silly fool for letting herself be taken in by his special brand of charm. She knew in her heart that she meant nothing to him, but she decided that for tonight at least that she was going to give herself up to the pleasure his touch was inflicting on her and be blowed with the consequences tomorrow would bring.

Dean's hands had started to move slowly over her back, tracing small patterns between her shoulder blades. She arched herself into him, not being able to control the response his touch was having on her fevered body. She wondered if he was aware of the power he had over her at this moment. She felt his lips roving over her forehead and had to control the slight shudder of delight which was trying to escape from her tingling body.

Feeling warm and vibrant, Mackenzie gave herself up to the heady sensations as they coursed throughout her body. She wanted this man, but how did you tell someone that you were attracted to them, that you wanted more? Dean had successfully sailed past all of her defenses, side stepping each and every one of them. She'd been attracted to him from the very first second, when he'd first come into her life.

It had been so long since she'd let anyone get this close to her, over three years, in fact. She was unsure of how to tell him. What if he said no to her once she'd told him? All of these thoughts were tumbling through her head as she gave herself up to the heady rapture of his touch.

Dean's lips had started to nuzzle her ear. She was going to go crazy if he didn't stop. Her body had started to throb with uncontrolled passion. *This is silly*, she thought. *How can a few casual embraces cause such a heated reaction? I've been held before and kissed before since Steve died, but never have I wanted any man to touch me in such an urgent way.* Mackenzie's body was on fire. Dean had unknowingly ignited the spark which was now in danger of spreading all over her body in an uncontrollable, all-consumable blaze. She knew only Dean could extinguish the mounting passion which was raging throughout her body.

Her mind flicked briefly back to Steve. She had to try to control this wild desire before it destroyed her completely. *It had been so easy with Steve*, she reasoned. Their whole relationship had just fallen into place, like pieces of a well-worn puzzle. With him, it had been so simple. She'd loved him dearly, but she'd never experienced this burning need to fulfill her desires with him as she did now. *Steve*, she thought sadly. He was truly gone from her life. It was now time for her to move on.

Dean stiffened, coming to an abrupt halt, thereby forcing her to do the same. Mackenzie looked up into his eyes, wondering why he'd stopped dancing. Confusion clouded her mind as she saw white hot anger lurking in the dark brown depths that were boring into her.

"What's the matter?" she asked bewildered by his sudden change of mood. She needed an explanation. Everything had been going so well. What had happened to change him back into this angry person who stood before her?

"My name's not Steve!" he told her between clenched teeth. "The least you could do was to get the name right, Mrs. Phillips."

He emphasised her surname, grinding it out, as if her name was an insect which he wanted to exterminate with the heel of his shoe.

"Dean . . . wait . . . please," she cried, unaware of the heads which had turned in their direction as she followed him from the room. She had to explain, to set him straight about Steve and the part he'd played in her life before it was too late. Maybe there was a chance for them to redeem the feelings which had been starting to grow stronger between them.

Outside, the stars were out in full, brilliant force, twinkling blissfully, unaware of the trouble which was about to erupt beneath them. It took Mackenzie a few seconds to locate Dean as her eyes had to become accustomed to the darkness which totally surrounded her. Also, the fresh air hit her like a blast from a gun, momentarily making her feel as if she was going to be sick. Taking a moment to get her bearings and to settle her heaving stomach, she found he was headed for the car park, probably wanting to make a hasty departure, needing to get as far away from her as he could.

Mackenzie called his name again, hoping he'd stop. The sound of her voice rang out in the darkness and seemed to her to disappear into nothingness. She tripped over the uneven ground, but was saved from falling flat on her face when she fell into a parked car.

Dean must have heard her because he stopped then and turned to look at her questioningly, frowning as she slowly covered the short distance which separated them from each other.

Even now as Mackenzie came to a reluctant stop before him, she was forced to admit to herself once again that she was no longer immune to his special brand of charm. *Oh Lord*, she thought wildly, *what have I gotten myself into here?* Feeling slightly apprehensive, she noticed that he was doing nothing to put her fears to rest. She felt as if she was about to be crucified, and all she could think about was how she'd felt when she'd been held in his arms.

Now that she was standing here in front of him, she seemed to have lost her will to speak. Just how did you tell someone who, until recently, you'd gone out of your way to avoid, that you wanted them? It didn't help that the only foundation for that wanting was based practically on a one night stand, and then he'd been thrust at her by someone else; someone who had been too drunk to dance with her. Mackenzie licked her lips nervously, not knowing exactly where to start.

Her soft brown eyes were trying unsuccessfully to communicate with his own brown orbs, but she could see that they were totally ignoring the turmoil she was feeling. Surely, he could see how distressed she was. *Perhaps he could*, she told herself, *but he just didn't care.* He was looking at her intently, waiting for her to say something. His face was obscured by shadows, so Mackenzie didn't know what thoughts were passing through his mind.

Licking her lips nervously, she started to tell him, but had to clear her voice and start again, "I just wanted to apologise for . . . for . . ." Mackenzie couldn't finish; she wasn't sure just what it was she wanted to say.

Dean, however, had no such qualms. He finished for her, delivering the words with a controlled coldness, "For what? For leading me on, for being a flirt, for being the kind of woman I detest?"

His words cut into her like a knife. They were sharp and pointed and were intended to wound her, but he was wrong, so very wrong. She wanted to lash out at him, to hurt him as much as his words had hurt her.

She looked up at him a trifle indignantly. "You think you're so smug, don't you?" Unabashed by his ominous glare, she continued, "You're so bigheaded! I suppose you think it's every woman's idea of heaven to sleep in your bed?" The alcohol had freed Mackenzie from any inhibitions which would have normally kept her emotions tightly stored under lock and key. She'd followed him outside, hoping he'd forgive her. Now she thought he could rot in hell before she'd ever lift a finger to help him again.

He further fuelled her rising temper by telling her confidently in a voice which was meant for her ears only, "I've had no complaints so far, Mrs. Phillips. Perhaps you'd care to sample some of my wares?" Upon saying this, Dean stepped forward, grabbing Mackenzie unawares, and pulled her roughly into his arms. His mouth came down onto hers, forcing her lips apart, allowing his tongue access to her mouth. It was a cruel kiss which lacked passion and caring, of any description. It wasn't the kiss of a lover but of a tyrant. Mackenzie stood passively, waiting for the kiss to end. It seemed to go on forever. This wasn't the way she'd pictured their first kiss would be.

Dean finally let her go, pushing her away from him as if she disgusted him. He told her in a voice which seemed hoarse with suppressed anger, "Go home to your husband. At least he still wants you," before adding caustically, "or does he?"

Mackenzie was incensed! How dare he bring Steve into this sordid mess? "Leave my husband out of this. He's . . . he's . . ." She couldn't bear to tell him now that Steve was dead. She thought he deserved better than to have his name thrown around in a game of insults between two people who, it seemed, would never be anything more to each other than enemies.

"He's what . . . incompetent? He can't be doing his job as a husband if you have to look elsewhere for company." He looked as if he was going to make a lunge for her again, but this time Mackenzie was ready for him. She lashed out at him, striking him savagely on the side of the face. The slap rang out in the darkness, echoing around the empty car park.

Rubbing the side of his face, Dean told her coldly, "That's quite a temper you've got there, Mrs. Phillips. I feel it would be remiss of me not to tell you to keep it under control in any future dealings you might have with me."

Mackenzie could see the anger glittering in his eyes like twin shafts of cold light as he cautioned her. Having delivered this message, he turned on his heel and walked away, leaving her standing in the darkness, watching him until he'd disappeared from sight.

Daylight found Mackenzie sitting in Jazz's kitchen, drinking a much-needed cup of coffee.

"Oh, boy," she told her, "that's better. Why didn't I listen to my mother's advice about the perils of drinking? Are you sure you don't have any aspirin?" Mackenzie's head was virtually pounding off the top of her head. She continued listlessly, "When I get my hands on Brian, I'm going to kill him. The rotter must have spiked my drinks . . . Well, not really, but they were a lot stronger than normal."

Jazz looked across at her friend. Mackenzie had been the last person in the world she'd expected to see standing on her doorstep earlier that morning. A feasible explanation still hadn't been given, but knowing Mackenzie as she did, Jazz knew it would only be a matter of time before Mackenzie opened up and told her the real reason for her unannounced visit.

"It must have been a corker of a party for you to be suffering this much," Jazz asked casually, trying to keep the laughter out of her voice.

"You can laugh. God, I feel terrible . . . I've really missed you, Jazz. Why did you have to move away?" Mackenzie said at last, finally getting around to the reason for her sudden visit.

Looking shrewdly across at her friend, Jazz said bluntly, "Now we get to the good part. Tell me, what really brought you here, Mac? Oh, I know you missed me and all that. I've missed you too, but that's not the only reason, is it? There's something else, isn't there?"

Mackenzie started to fidget, moving around in her chair and fingering the rim of the coffee cup she held loosely in her hands. Suddenly, she couldn't look her friend in the eye. Speech had suddenly deserted her. The trouble was she didn't know where to start. How do you tell someone that you made a horrible mess of a would-be blossoming relationship all because of one silly mistake?

"Ah! I knew I was right. You're displaying all of the symptoms of a woman with a secret. Come on, out with it before I die of curiosity."

"You called him Steve? Wow! No wonder he went off at you. Mackenzie, how could you be so stupid? No man would like to be reminded of a dead husband, especially when he's trying to make a move on you."

Mackenzie had just related most of the story of her disastrous night out. She felt better for having told someone as she knew she would. Jazz had listened quietly, probably because she was totally dumbfounded over the antics of her irresponsible friend when it came to her dealings with members of the opposite sex.

"He doesn't know that Steve is dead." Mackenzie muttered simply. She could see the visible reaction this late piece of news was causing on her friend's face. Utter disbelief was etched in every curve, letting Mackenzie know exactly what thoughts must be cascading through her head.

"What?" she exclaimed. "What do you mean he doesn't know Steve is dead? Surely he's heard from someone!" Jazz couldn't believe

the stupidity of her friend. Mackenzie looked as if she was going to
burst into tears at any moment, but Jazz was too dumbfounded to
take this minor detail into account.

"Why haven't you told him? Talk about a comedy of errors.
Mackenzie, this is priceless. Only you could get yourself into a mess
like this." Jazz was looking at her friend intently. Some of her initial
shock was wearing off, and she was able to rationalise the situation
a little better.

"I don't know," Mackenzie confessed miserably. She was a
bit taken aback by Jazz's apparent lack of concern. She was the
one person in the world that she thought would understand the
feelings which were coursing throughout her tormented body at the
moment. It seemed to Mackenzie that all of her sympathy was for
Dean.

"Well, you know what you have to do, don't you?" Jazz told her
firmly.

Mackenzie eyed her friend suspiciously. "What?" she asked
cautiously, afraid that she already knew the answer to her
question.

"You have to tell him. The poor man is probably feeling like
hell," Jazz said simply.

"And just how, pray tell, am I supposed to do that? I suppose
you think I should just walk up to him and say casually, 'By the
way, Dean, did I ever tell you that Steve, my husband, is dead? No?
Oh, how silly of me, it must have slipped my mind.'" Mackenzie's
retort was slightly caustic, but she didn't care. She was past
caring. Her palms had suddenly gone damp, and her stomach had
started to heave. "Oh, no," she wailed, making a mad dash for the
bathroom. "I'm going to be sick."

Mackenzie's hangover put a stop to any further conversation
between them. She was sick for the rest of the day. Jazz came into

the bedroom and checked on her from time to time, but for the most part, she slept, and for that, she was grateful. Every time she woke up, she was sick. This was the weirdest hangover she'd ever had.

"Hey, sunshine, wake up," Jazz was standing in the bedroom doorway, sipping a cup of coffee.

"Mmm, that smells wonderful," Mackenzie commented as the fresh aroma of the coffee filled her nostrils. "Is there any more?"

"Heaps. Are you sure you can keep it down?" Jazz mused as she took in the pale features of her friend.

"No, but I'll try. I do feel a lot better than I did before. I'm definitely going to kill Brian when I see him," Mackenzie assured her friend as she cautiously swung her long shapely legs over the side of the bed.

"So far, so good," Jazz told her, still not being able to keep the smile out of her voice.

"What's so funny?" Mackenzie wanted to know. "You definitely have a warped sense of humour. Remind me never to come to you again with my problems. I'd get more sympathy from the devil himself."

"Funny you should say that," she commented slowly.

Mackenzie's head shot up as she quickly scanned her friend's face. This untimely action made her cringe, and she had to hold her head as another wave of dizziness washed over her again.

"Jazz, what have you done?" Mackenzie's voice was full of the trepidation she was feeling, and her stomach started to contract again, but not from sickness, but from full-blown fear. It took a moment or two for the full implication of Jazz's actions to completely sink in. Mackenzie lay on her back, covering her eyes with her hands. She was beyond words. There wasn't anything left to say. She was doomed. How on earth was she ever going to face him now?

"Yes, I did," Jazz answered the unasked question which she could see lurking in her friend's eyes. "And might I add that I was right."

However, Jazz didn't tell her friend how nervous she'd been about getting in touch with Dean. Her own husband had told her not to meddle, telling her that they had to work it out for themselves. Luckily, Jazz had ignored this advice and had gone ahead putting her plan into action.

In fact, Jazz had made a few calls, omitting, of course, that Mackenzie was here with her, suffering from a very severe bout of lovesickness. She'd rung Dean on the pretense of finding out if he was happy with the house. She'd deftly swung the conversation around to Mackenzie, telling him what a great pity it was that she'd been widowed at such a young age. Gratification had flooded her at the absolute silence, which had followed her carefully orchestrated, casual remark. When he'd finally spoken, it was to tell her that he'd been unaware of Mackenzie's marital status. Jazz could hear the pain in his voice, and her heart had gone out to him.

Her other calls also fell on fertile ground. Jazz was regaled with some very interesting tidbits about the antics of her friend and the new deputy head. It seemed that Mackenzie had been singled out to work with Dean in an effort to make his transition into the school a smooth, pleasant one. This idea had to be scraped, however, due to a heated argument which took place between the two of them on his very first day. Jazz wondered with mounting curiosity just what had happened over the weekend to fuel this argument. It wasn't like Mackenzie to fight with anyone. Something must have triggered off the friction between them, and Jazz meant to find out before this day ended.

Since that day, apparently, they'd been avoiding each other like the plague. They were barely courteous when forced into each other's company. Without knowing it, they'd become the talk of the school, although Jazz was assured none of the talk had been malicious in any way. Everyone wanted Mackenzie and Dean to get together; it seemed the only two people who were oblivious to this fact were Mackenzie and Dean themselves. Jazz found herself wondering if anyone at the school had come to the conclusion that they were neighbours. She fervently hoped that there was still a fighting chance for their flagging relationship to grow and flourish into something more lasting and real.

Underneath all of her light banter, Jazz was genuinely concerned about the welfare of her friend. She wanted Mackenzie to move on with her life. She'd been stagnating for far too long. Mourning over a man who was long gone wasn't healthy as far as she was concerned. She could only hide herself away from the human race for so long. Hopefully, meeting Dean had brought her back from the deep void which had been her hiding place for the last three years. Jazz knew she'd have to try appealing to Mackenzie's logical side, if it still existed, in the hope of getting her to see the truth which was right before her eyes.

"Come on, let's go and have that coffee. You're not off the hook just yet." Jazz wasn't prepared to let the subject of Dean rest. From what she could gather from the bits of information she was slowly being fed, her friend had virtually run away from home to escape the consequences of her actions of the night before. Her fear of facing Dean stemmed from the mental torture that he was capable of inflicting on her merely by his presence.

Jazz decided it was time she set Mackenzie straight about a few home truths. She was convinced now was the time. Some things just weren't obvious until they'd been pointed out. She fervently hoped Mackenzie would realise this when she'd finished what she was about to say.

Jazz wasn't a person who was known for holding things back; when she had something to say, she usually came straight out and said it. Never-the-less, she felt a small amount of trepidation as she prepared to say what she felt. Her only saving grace was that it was coming from her heart. Mackenzie was her best friend, and she hated to see her hurting. She felt it was her duty to have her say. She knew if the situation was reversed, Mackenzie wouldn't hesitate to do the same thing for her.

"Dean is flesh and blood," she told Mackenzie as a way of starting, then continued, "Steve is only a memory." Jazz knew this was a low blow, but she wanted to jolt Mackenzie out of the self-imposed monastic lifestyle that she'd been living. She carefully placed a photograph of Steve onto the table, placing it directly in front of her friend. Mackenzie looked up at her questioningly, wondering what was going on. "You have to choose now, Mackenzie." Jazz's voice trailed away into silence as she watched Mackenzie reach out automatically to take the photograph which had been placed before her.

Mackenzie realised Jazz was giving her an ultimatum. She was making her choose between Steve and Dean. A slow smile covered her trembling lips as she compared the two men. *They are so different*, she thought sadly. Steve had been like a warm, sunny afternoon when you were sitting inside, safe and secure. He'd been a wonderful, loving husband, in fact, everything she thought she'd ever wanted in a relationship. Dean, on the other hand, was like a raging forest fire which consumed everything in its path. He was the most incredible man she'd ever met. Her feelings were uncontrollable when she was near him. She was always wanting to touch him, to be closer to him than she had a right to be. Her feelings overwhelmed her when she was in his presence. This had never happened to her before. Everyone else paled by comparison, everyone, even Steve. She realised then that part of her reluctance to let her feelings show probably stemmed from guilt. She understood that she'd grown a lot in the past three years and had probably outgrown Steve. Passing her fingers slowly over the handsome features depicted in the photograph, she was reminded yet again of the love they'd shared. She could feel a lump forming in the back of her throat as she tried to suppress the emotion she was starting to feel.

"Mackenzie," Jazz broke in, capturing her friend's attention once again, waiting for her to put the photograph down. When she had her friend's attention, she asked simply, "How did that feel?"

Confusion clouded Mackenzie's drawn features as she tried to bring herself back to the present and concentrate on Jazz's question. "What?" she asked, somewhat confused as she tried to break away from the memories of the past.

"I asked how it felt. Did it thrill you to the depths of your being to touch that photograph? Did it take your breath away? Are you starting to tingle with suppressed anticipation wondering what might happen next?"

"Why are you doing this to me? I thought we were friends." Mackenzie was struggling with the words. Her throat was constricted with unshed tears.

"Why am I doing this? Because I'm your friend . . . your best friend, and I want you to wake up to yourself before it's too late." Jazz snatched the photograph of Steve out of Mackenzie's unresisting grasp and flung it into the corner, where contact with the floor shattered the glass, "See that didn't hurt him a bit because he's dead, Mackenzie. He's dead. He's not flesh and blood anymore, so you can stop waiting for him to come home. He's gone . . . dead and buried."

"Stop it!" Mackenzie pleaded. Her voice had begun to shake. She'd listened to enough. She wanted Jazz to stop. This wasn't fair; she knew Steve wasn't coming back . . . Who knew that better than her.

"I'll stop when you stop feeling sorry for yourself, but until then, I'm going to keep on your back." Jazz had just about had enough. She was going to have her say and be blowed with the consequences.

She continued, totally ignoring the shimmer of tears which she could see brimming behind the rims of Mackenzie's large brown eyes. "I've sat back for the last three years and watched you throw your life away on a ghost. Dean Ashleigh is not a ghost. He's flesh and blood . . . and available. I'd bet everything I own that he's interested in you. In fact, I'd go so far as to say that he's more than interested in you."

"He's involved with someone already. What do you want me to do? Stand in line! And I'll tell you something else, she's flesh and blood too. I've seen her coming and going from your place . . . er, his place," Mackenzie told Jazz in no uncertain terms. "So if he's so interested, who is the other woman?"

"I don't believe it," Jazz told her, totally confused by this piece of news.

"He's probably sincere about the brunette as well," Mackenzie said waspishly, put out by the fact that Jazz seemed to be siding with Dean. She knew he wasn't interested in her. It was only a fantasy conjured up in her own feeble mind.

"Oh, I've had enough of this," Jazz jumped up and started pacing across the kitchen floor. She looked like a lioness that was about to pounce on its prey. "When are you going to admit to yourself that you like this damn man?" When Mackenzie would have interrupted, she held up her hand, effectively silencing her.

"It's true, but you're too stubborn to admit it, even to yourself," she went on dramatically, walking around the table, raising her arms every now and again to provide an extra bit of emphasis for the points she was trying to make.

"You side step each other like you have the plague, but regardless of what you say or think, it's as plain as the nose on Pinocchio's face that you two are attracted to each other. You both covertly watch each other when you think no one else is watching you."

"How do you know all of this? It sounds like a lot of rubbish to me," Mackenzie broke in at last, wanting some answers of her own. It was disquieting to think that her casual glances in Dean's direction had been catalogued and passed on to everyone in the school. She'd thought she was being discreet.

"I've got my sources, but you know that already," Jazz answered shortly, continuing before her friend could try to side track her again, "All of the signs are there, Mackenzie, for everyone else to see, so why can't you see what's right before your eyes . . . or are you purposely avoiding him?"

Mackenzie flashed her a look which would have melted an iceberg, but Jazz barged on, knowing now that she'd finally hit a nerve. "Hey, that's it, isn't it? You do like him, don't you? Well, if that's the case, what's with all this cloak-and-dagger stuff?"

Jazz had come to stand beside Mackenzie. She ran her hand slowly over her friend's arm, then casually ran the tips of her fingers along the side of her face. "Can Steve do that anymore, Mackenzie?" she said softly. "Can he make your nerve endings turn to jelly the way Dean's touch does? Can you honestly look me in the eye and tell me you're not the slightest bit interested in the new deputy head? Because if you can, I'll leave you alone."

"What . . . what do you mean?" Mackenzie stammered, not quite being able to meet Jazz's inquisitive stare. She ran her tongue over her lips which had suddenly gone very dry.

"You know exactly what I mean." Jazz stood her ground. Mackenzie had to let go of a memory. Until she did this, she'd be unable to move on. Steve's memory would always be in the way. She had to be made to understand that now was the time to grab life with both hands and run with it.

"What do you want me to say?" Mackenzie threw at her tormentor caustically. "That Dean only has to look at me and I turn into a quivering mess or that when we danced last night I completely lost my head?"

"What about your heart?" Jazz asked simply.

Mackenzie started to cry as she stammered softly, "That too."

"Well, at least that's a step in the right direction," Jazz commented, satisfied that her incessant probing had finally found fertile ground.

The Tropic of Capricorn passes through Rockhampton
on the south side.

The Tropic of Capricorn plus information centre
on Gladstone Road South Rockhampton.

Tropic of Capricorn spire

One of the many bulls that can be found around Rockhampton.
Rockhampton is known as "The Beef Capital" of Queensland.

This lovely arrangement of flowers in the shape of a floral clock
can be seen at the Botanical Gardens.

Sitting on the steps of the old Customs House which was built in 1898-1901 in a Classis Rivival style with a Greek Corinthian influence.

On the boardwalk with the Fitzroy River in the background.
Enjoying each other's company.

Dean and Mackenzie.

Standing on the old bridge with the Criterion Hotel in the background.
Room 22 is said to be haunted by a chambermaid who committed
suicide because of a broken heart. It is said that she can sometimes
be heard in this room.

Side view of the Criterion from Denham Street. Built in 1889
in Neo Classic Revival Style with a French influence.
Known as "The Cri" to locals.

Dean and Mackenzie enjoying a drink at the Cri
after a day of sightseeing.

Looking towards the man-made landscape of 3 waterfalls and lagoon at the Kershaw Gardens. The scene is completed by the palm trees that surround the lagoon.

CHAPTER FOUR

"I don't know if this was such a good idea," Mackenzie was clearly agitated as she stepped from the passenger side of Jazz's car. They had just driven from the Sunshine Coast, arriving at Mackenzie's place in the middle of the day. Mackenzie found she was looking around wearily for signs of Dean.

"It's alright, I'll protect you from your big, bad neighbour," Jazz quipped. Seeing the look of absolute scorn on Mackenzie's face, she smilingly added, "Well, you're being silly. For one thing he'll be at work."

"I suppose you think that's funny, don't you?" Mackenzie threw a look of pure contempt at her travelling companion, although if she was going to be completely honest with herself, she had to admit that she was being just a little paranoid where Dean was concerned. The thought of Jazz protecting her brought a smile to her stiff lips and a sparkle to her eyes. She realised sadly that it had been far too long since she'd really laughed.

"Well, at least it made you smile," she was told candidly.

"I have been a bit of a wet blanket, haven't I?" Mackenzie admitted ruefully. "I don't know why you put up with me."

"Because you're my best friend," Jazz answered simply, giving Mackenzie a direct stare before reverting to her carefree attitude of a few moments ago. "As for the other, well, nobody's perfect. Come on, let's go inside, I'm dying for a cup of coffee."

"Mmm, that's better," Jazz told Mackenzie as she stretched out on the lounge chair, cradling a cup of hot coffee in the palm of her hands.

They had driven nonstop from Jazz's home since she'd reasoned that Mackenzie would need more clothes other than the hastily packed wardrobe that she'd arrived with three days ago.

Mackenzie was nervously looking at the clock as she paced the floor. The constant ticking of the second hand was letting her know that if they stayed any longer, they'd risk bumping into Dean when he arrived home from school. She'd tried sitting still, but her stomach was being torn apart by nerves.

"Jazz," she yelled for the third time, "when are you going to be ready to leave? If we don't leave soon, we're going to run into all of the afternoon traffic." She'd been ready for hours, but Jazz was lagging. It never occurred to Mackenzie that her friend was deliberately trying to waste time.

"Yes, I know. I'm sorry, but I'm feeling a bit squeamish in the stomach. If you're worried about Dean Ashleigh coming over, I'm sure you're the last person he wants to see anyway." Jazz was starting to get worried also, but for different reasons. Perhaps Rob had been right, and she should have minded her own business. She reasoned with herself that if he didn't turn up, she'd have her answer as well. If that turned out to be the case, she'd do everything in her power to help Mackenzie get over her love for this man.

Mackenzie walked into the bedroom to find Jazz sitting on the side of the bed. She looked a bit pale and was holding her head in her hands.

"Are you alright, Jazz?" Mackenzie came into the room, feeling a bit guilty. She'd been so obsessed with her own problems that she'd failed to notice that her friend wasn't well.

"Yes, I'm probably just tired or something."

"Hey, is there something that you're not telling me?" Mackenzie asked her friend.

"What?" Jazz's eyes flew to Mackenzie's face, hoping her glance would not confirm her fears. Had Mackenzie guessed her elaborate plan? She was saved from answering any more of Mackenzie's queries as a loud banging was heard at the front door, followed by a voice that Mackenzie knew only too well.

"Mackenzie," she heard the uncertainty in Dean's voice as he called out to her.

"Oh, no! Jazz, he's here. What am I going to do?" Mackenzie whispered. Her heart was beating at an alarming rate as she looked around the room trying to figure out how she could escape the confrontation which was in front of her.

She continued, "Go out there. Tell him something, anything. Tell him you came up here to get me some things."

Jazz could see the panic etched into the fine lines of her friend's face. She couldn't stop the slight smile from covering her heart-shaped face as she said, "Get out there. Let's get this mess cleared up once and for all so that I can go home."

Mackenzie felt like a child who was about to be punished. Jazz had to practically push her through the door and down the hallway towards the front door.

"It's about time you got here. I was running out of excuses as to why we couldn't leave. I wasn't sure how much longer I could delay our departure," Jazz told Dean as she searched his face, hoping she'd made the right decision on Mackenzie's behalf.

Mackenzie couldn't believe her ears. They were talking as if they both knew what was going on. She looked from one to the other, trying to fathom out exactly what was happening.

"I've just been told about your message. Some damn fool put the piece of paper on my desk, thinking I'd see it, but it got lost under all of the clutter," came his quick response. "I got here as soon as I could." His mind returned momentarily to the scene he'd just left. He knew, come tomorrow, he'd have some heartfelt apologies to make to some very startled people.

"I can't believe you did this," Mackenzie told Jazz. She'd paled and had started to visibly shake as the reality of what was happening finally hit her, "I thought you were my friend."

"Don't blame Jazz. I talked her into helping me. I just wasn't sure of the details," Dean told her, taking control of the situation.

"You asked Jazz about me?" Mackenzie couldn't believe it. He actually had the audacity to approach her best friend, looking for information about her, and judging by his appearance in her home, he'd found it.

"When?" she snapped waspishly at him. She couldn't help it, she was starting to bristle. Some of her trepidation at seeing Dean was starting to recede as another emotion rose to the surface of her consciousness to take its place.

"On Sunday," he answered simply, knowing further explanations were going to be necessary before he was let off this particular hook.

"You rang Jazz? Why?" she wanted to know.

Jazz had been sitting quietly, taking in the scene before her. Talk about a comedy of errors. If the situation before her wasn't so serious, she'd be laughing at the both of them. She could see, as an outsider, that the two people standing before her had very deep feelings for each other. All they had to do was admit it to each other. She already knew they'd admitted it to themselves.

"Hang on, Mackenzie, you've got it all wrong. I rang him. If you'd calm down for a minute, you'd remember that I told you already. Don't give me that wounded puppy look because it's a good thing I did, the poor man was half out of his mind, worrying about you," Jazz piped in, wanting to set the record straight. The last thing Dean needed at this time was to have Mackenzie blasting him for doing nothing other than loving her.

Mackenzie was staring at them both; she was momentarily lost for words as she tried to digest the information Jazz had given her.

Taking advantage of the situation, Dean quickly said, "Well, you wouldn't tell me anything about yourself. What was I supposed to do? How do you think I felt when Jazz told me your husband was dead? I didn't know, I mean, he could have been away, but the thing that I don't understand, if your husband is dead, who was it you were going to meet the other day? Sue said Steve rang you . . ." His voice trailed off as the confusion became too much for him to contemplate. He was gazing down at her, waiting for answers, but he was sure he was going to be bombarded with an abusive torrent any time now.

Confusion clouded Mackenzie's mind as she tried to piece together all of the things that he'd said to her. She knew she was to blame for a lot of the misunderstanding that had flowed between them, but at the time, her intentions had been pure. She hadn't wanted to drag Steve's name into a sordid affair. He meant more to her than that. The timing had always been wrong, she hadn't wanted to use Steve as a buffer, but she wasn't sure how to explain this fact to the man who now stood before her.

Her voice was probably harsher than she intended as she told him, "If you felt you couldn't ask me, why didn't you just ask someone at school! My life is an open book. I'm sure any number of people would've been only too happy to fill in any gaps for you."

"I wasn't going to ask total strangers to tell me about you, and it seemed every time I tried to talk to you, we'd end up having an argument. Why couldn't you have told me, Mackenzie?"

Looking up at him, Mackenzie answered apprehensively, "I don't know. In the beginning, it didn't really matter that you didn't know Steve was dead. I mean . . . everyone knows . . . it's not a closely guarded secret or anything. My marital status isn't something I automatically inject into the conversation."

"But you must have suspected how I felt about you," he asked her as he distractedly ran his hands through his hair. Then he continued, "Do you have any idea what a louse I thought of myself because of my feelings for you? The other night at the hotel, I overstepped the mark completely. I should have stayed away but . . ." He shrugged his shoulders and left the rest of his sentence unsaid, letting Mackenzie draw her own conclusions as to what he was trying to say. He realised he'd probably said too much already.

"Oh!" was all that Mackenzie could think of to say as she realised the full implication of his words. She walked over to the lounge chair, needing to sit down because suddenly her legs felt as if they were about to buckle beneath her.

"You must think I'm an absolute monster for putting you through all of this. Will you forgive me?" Dean deeply regretted the events of the last few days, wishing fervently that he had the power to turn back the clock. He'd wipe their slate completely clean and start from the very first time he'd set eyes on her. To his utter astonishment, he saw tears forming in her eyes, tears which she made no effort to hide.

Unable to speak, Mackenzie merely nodded her head. This chain of events was too much for her to take in. This man cared for her, and she'd very nearly ruined any chance of happiness they might have had because of a silly misunderstanding that had been allowed to fester and get totally out of control.

Dean knelt on the floor in front of her. He gently gathered her into his arms and cradled her head on his broad shoulder. This was too much for Mackenzie. She started sobbing, needing the release that only tears could bring for so many of the things that had happened over the past few days.

Jazz looked on, totally confident that the two of them would now be able to work everything out between them. She could see that her friend was in good hands. Not wanting to be in the way, she silently slipped away. She felt a bit like a patron saint that had just done a good deed. Her job was done, now it was up to Dean and Mackenzie.

"Mackenzie," Dean murmured softly into the soft contours of her neck as she tried unsuccessfully to control her crying, "sweetheart, I know I'm probably jumping the gun telling you this, but just so there are no more misunderstandings between us . . . I'm in love with you . . . I just wanted you to know. You don't have to say anything but . . ." This was as much as Dean was able to say because Mackenzie turned her head and softly covered his lips with her own, letting her action speak for her before she finally whispered, "I love you too."

The kiss they shared deepened as their mutual desire for each other flared to overcome the turmoil that had kept them apart for so long.

Dean's embrace changed from one of concern to one of passion as he gathered Mackenzie more securely into his masculine grasp.

For her part, Mackenzie slid out of her chair, bringing her soft body up against the hard length of Dean's. Their bodies fused together as they knelt on the floor. Her arms found their way around his neck, bringing their heated bodies together. Their embrace felt so right, so natural. This was where they both were meant to be.

Mackenzie revelled in the sensual feel of Dean's lips against her own, rousing her sleeping body to full alertness once again. She strained against him, needing to feel the hard contours of his masculine body against her own. Dean's tongue tantalised her lips, the inside of her mouth; he played with the line of her teeth, wanting to investigate and seek out all of the sweetness that she was offering him.

In her turn, Mackenzie had started to stimulate him by returning his kisses with a passionate abandonment that left her breathless. She'd wondered for so long how it would feel to kiss Dean, to have him kiss her, to savour the heady sensation of his body touching hers in an intimate way. Her body and mind was parched of affection, and she was like someone grasping at a lifeline that had been offered to her.

Her expectations of their first kiss surpassed all of her wildest dreams. Giving herself up to the intoxicating sensations which were running rampant throughout her body was wonderful, she gave a gasp of pure delight as Dean covered her face with a succession of small sharp kisses, which ultimately led him to the lobe of one of her ears, where he bestowed a series of lingering kisses, making himself familiar with the contours of her face, before he blazed a trail of feathered kisses down the nape of her neck where an erratic pulse was beating an insistent tattoo. She shivered in pure delight, loving the erotic sensation that his touch was creating all over her fevered body. She wantonly tried to pull him closer, loving the hard strength of him as he moved against her.

She felt bereft when Dean stopped kissing her, not wanting him to stop. She wanted to be able to touch him, to savour the lingering scent of his masculine body, to run her fingers through his hair which had fallen over his forehead, giving him an almost boyish look.

Looking up at him questioningly, through eyes that were still glazed with passion, she saw that he was contemplating her with a heartwarming gaze, which did nothing to slow the wild beating of her heart. Her voice sounded breathless as she asked slowly, "Dean, what's wrong?"

"Nothing's wrong, my love, everything's fine, perfect in fact, but if I don't stop kissing you now, I won't be able to stop myself from making love to you right here on the floor." His breath was coming in short bursts as if he was having difficulty breathing. "I want the first time we make love to be free from doubt for the both of us. Tell me you understand. I don't know why, but it's important to me. I don't want anything to go wrong."

The sincerity in Dean's voice made Mackenzie realise that he was correct, although her body still clamoured for his touch. She knew she still had a lot to learn about him, but her heightened senses would have welcomed his love making. The thought of him making love to her brought a warm flush to her cheeks, and her body shivered with the anticipation of his intimate touch, which she sought to hide by lowering her head into his chest.

"Hey, what's this?" he wanted to know. Cupping her chin in his strong capable fingers, he raised her face so that he could look again into her dreamy brown eyes. His smile told her he understood the feelings which were coursing throughout her fevered body, for he whispered softly, "It's not completely one-sided you know. I'm far from immune to your special brand of charm either. Come on, let's get up off the floor before you talk me into changing my mind. When you look at me with those big, sexy eyes, I don't think I could deny you anything."

"You make me sound like a sex maniac," she told him demurely as they both got unsteadily to their feet. Now that her thinking was returning to normal and her head was starting to clear from the cloud of passion that had enveloped it, she realised he was probably right.

"One can only hope," he grinned down at her, giving her a quick kiss and a hug as he looked around the room. "Hey, where's Jazz?"

"Is her car outside?" Mackenzie asked as she headed towards the front door to see if Jazz's car was still parked in the driveway. She wasn't at all surprised to find that the vehicle was missing. She added, "Nope, it's gone. She must have left when we were busy,"

"Well, I guess that means we're on our own. Does that mean she trusts me with you? Maybe she's just gone to get some food. I don't know about you, but I'm absolutely starving," Dean told her, rubbing his stomach. He realised that he hadn't eaten very much over the last couple of days. He turned to Mackenzie asking, "Do you want to go out for something?"

Mackenzie smiled across at him, thinking she must remember to phone Jazz tomorrow and thank her for being the catalyst which finally brought her to her senses as far as Dean was concerned.

"I guess so," she answered simply. It seemed so strange and yet so natural to Mackenzie that they were standing here talking, making plans as simple as going out for a bite to eat. Now that there was some distance between them, Mackenzie's mind had started to conjure up images that would not let her be. For instance, if he did truly love her, then who was the other woman in his life?

Was he the kind of man who professed his undying love to every woman he took up with? *All she had to rely on was his word, she thought sadly.* She didn't know enough about him to know if he was after a conquest or a stable relationship.

"I can almost hear the wheels turning inside that pretty head of yours," he said lightly, "but I've got a feeling you're not thinking pretty thoughts. Come on, out with it before you let whatever it is fester, and we both live to regret it."

Mackenzie sighed. She wasn't sure if she was ready to talk to him about her innermost thoughts. If she was wrong, he would be hurt, not to mention angry; and if she was correct, she wasn't sure if this was the right time to delve into emotional quicksand when she wasn't thinking with a clear head. She was sure she'd be pulled in way over her head.

Anyway, she thought to herself, *this was a problem that all couples faced when they first met.* Why should she think that their relationship would be any different from the problems faced by other couples? The only way to find out was to go forward, not backward. This was a learning time for the both of them, and she vowed that she'd do her homework properly before she made any rash decisions.

"Mackenzie," Dean came to stand beside her; he had a puzzled expression on his lean face. He rested his hands lightly on her slim shoulders, kneading her skin slowly with the tips of his fingers, "Sweetheart, talk to me. I don't want any secrets between us. That's how relationships die."

"Do we have a relationship, Dean?" Mackenzie wanted to know simply.

"We have the start of one. Whether it grows or dies, depends on the both of us or how much of ourselves we put into it. For my part, I want it to grow and flourish. Is that what's been bothering you, that I might just be another male on the prowl with the only thought on my mind being how I might get you into bed?"

"The thought did cross my mind," she answered him candidly but tacked on quickly when she saw the frown starting to form on his tanned brow, "but then I came to the same conclusion that you did about working on a relationship if you want it to work." She slid her arms around his neck, pulling him closer to her body, loving how just being near him had a tantalising effect on her senses. Her heart was starting to pound, and her body had started to tingle in delicious anticipation. All in all, it was a very pleasing sensation.

"Well, I'm glad we finally agree on something," he told her as he brought his lips down to meet hers. Mackenzie opened herself up to him, rejoicing in the rhapsody that his nearness was reviving in her.

"Oh, Dean," she murmured, when she could finally speak. Her breathing was laboured, and she had to drag the air into her lungs. Resting her head against his chest, she was gratified to hear his own heart was beating rapidly against her flushed cheek. The constant tattoo made her feel secure; it gave her hope for their future life together.

Dean expelled his breath slowly; Mackenzie's body was trembling as he held her in his arms.

"Mackenzie," Dean said tentatively as he reluctantly moved his upper body away from her so that he could look down into her face to judge the reaction of his next words. "I didn't think I'd ever hear myself say these words to a beautiful woman, but if we don't stop, I'm going to lose control. This is the second time in one day. God, I must be going crazy asking you to stop kissing me."

Mackenzie smiled. "I know you're right, but I can't seem to stop myself. You're going to have to leave if you want me to stop touching you." Seeing the comical look that washed over his face, she added as an afterthought, "Okay, look, we both need to get cleaned up, so how about we retire to our respective homes, then if you want too, you can come back over here for dinner, and I promise you we can talk."

"Heavens, a truly liberated woman. What next?" he joked as he pulled his tie from around his neck where it had been hanging. "I do feel rather grotty at that. Okay, you win. I'll be back in one hour. By the way, do you like pizza?" Seeing Mackenzie's affirmative nod, he continued, "Good, I'll order us a large one." Upon saying this, he gave her a quick, firm kiss, and then he was gone.

Mackenzie sadly watched him walk through the front door. She wanted to call him back because she felt as if a large part of her had just walked out with him. She tried to gather herself into action, but instead she went and sat down on one of the lounge chairs. She realised that today she'd taken a very large step forward, but the trouble with moving on usually meant that some things had to be left behind.

Looking around her lounge room, Mackenzie's mind registered bits and pieces which she could associate with the various phases of her life. Photos lined one entire wall, depicting various events in her life that she'd deemed worthy of special remembrance. There were knick-knacks gathering dust in a wall unit, which she loved because of the special significance to certain periods in her life. These things were special to Mackenzie, but she realised sadly that to anyone else they'd seem silly, perhaps even childish. If she was to enter into a relationship with Dean, how would he feel about her trinkets, especially the ones that Steve had given her? Would he understand her desire to keep them, or would he want her to get rid of them? Some of those phases had been shared with Steve, others had been hard won through perseverance and sheer determination after Steve had died. Now it seemed she was about to start another phase, and she had to admit, she was just a little scared. What if she failed? She'd held the love of a very good man. Was it feasible that she could be so lucky a second time? Dean told her that he loved her, but did that necessarily mean that he wanted a lifelong commitment? Did he want any of the traditional things, like marriage and children, things that usually went hand in hand with a relationship? Mackenzie knew these days, when couples entered into a commitment, they did so lightly, with the knowledge that the arrangement could be revoked at any time if it failed. She wondered if her desire for Dean stemmed from a purely physical need. Once that need had been filled, would she still want him to be a part of her life? She believed in marriage, knowing she wanted all of the things that a lot of people today saw as being unnecessary. How did Dean feel about marriage? Did he share her views, or would they clash on this subject too? They'd have to talk about so many things, some of which, on the surface, seemed to hold very little importance, but they were really bones of contention to Mackenzie.

Mackenzie wondered if he'd want her to suppress her memories of Steve because she wasn't sure if she could do that. He'd been a good part of her life, and his memory deserved better treatment from her than to be casually thrown away in such a haphazard way. Dean would have to accept that she'd been in a secure relationship, which the unrelenting hand of death had stopped so savagely.

Knowing she had a big decision to make which would undoubtedly change the way in which she lived her life, Mackenzie weighed up the pros and cons of starting a relationship with Dean.

Do you like him? she asked herself, already knowing the answer to her silly question. *Well then, what's the problem?* she prompted herself. *Why are you putting up defenses that are ultimately going to cause problems later on?*

I don't want to cause any problems, she answered herself, confused by her own stupidity, *but I need to be sure that this all-consuming need for Dean is returned. I guess when it is all boiled down, I need to feel that I'm doing the right thing.* The word "guilt" rang out in her brain, and she realised that her problems stemmed from a sense of guilt, but that is the most ridiculous reason you could come up with. *Why guilt, for heaven's sake! Steve is dead; you're a widow and have been for more than three years. You've been out with other men. Why didn't you feel guilty about your association with any of them? I didn't care about any of them,* she told herself caustically. *I didn't have these overpowering yearnings that threatened to destroy my powers of reason when I was with them. I was in control, but now, I feel lost in a sea of uncertainty.*

Well, she continued to herself, *you are going to have to learn to live with these feelings and deal with them. The simple truth is that you're in love with Dean. You're in way over your head, and that scares you because you can't predict what's in store for you. When he comes back, talk to him about your fears. Maybe he's a bit apprehensive too. Knowing you hasn't been a walk in the park for him either. You've fought him every step of the way. Now it's time to give in. If he didn't care, he would have stopped trying ages ago.*

Mackenzie glanced over at the clock and was appalled to see how much time she'd wasted. "Oh my god!" she yelled as she jumped out of the chair. Dean would be back at any minute, and she desperately wanted to be ready for him. She started to peel off her clothes as she made her way to the bathroom. Damn, she'd never be ready on time, and she'd wanted to look her best at least once while in his company.

She was just putting the finishing touches to her appearance when she heard him coming up the front steps. "Come in." she called. "I won't be long."

She'd wanted to appear casual and not overdressed, but at the same time, she'd wanted to look good for him. She'd chosen blue jeans that hugged her body and emphasised her shapely long legs. To complete her outfit, she wore a deep blue knitted top which she knew suited her colouring and also brought out the highlights in her hair. She slipped her feet into sandals, hoping he'd like the completed picture. She only had enough time to put her hair up into a plait, leaving a few tendrils around her face which helped to soften her features. She decided against wearing any make-up, mainly because she'd run out of time, but also because as a rule, she usually chose not to wear face paint, opting instead for a more natural look. She'd sprayed herself with a light perfume, loving the fragrance of musk that immediately permeated the room.

She was nervous as she made her way down the hallway into the lounge. She spied him sitting casually on one of the comfortable chairs that lined one wall. She told him nervously, "I wasn't sure what to wear. It looks like I made the correct choice."

Dean was dressed in a similar fashion to herself. The blue jeans which hugged his body made him look incredibly sexy as far as Mackenzie was concerned. He'd shaved, and she could see that some of the worry lines had disappeared from around his eyes and mouth. She could smell his cologne and breathed it in deeply, filling her lungs, loving the aroma of him that filled her nostrils. She would always associate the smell of spices with him now.

"You look great," he told her as he looked across the room at her appreciatively. He covered the distance between them in a few steps, taking Mackenzie into his strong embrace. He planted a quick kiss onto her soft, willing lips, then told her simply, "If I don't get something to eat soon, I'm going to pass out. Come on, let's eat." Taking her hand in his strong, capable grasp, he guided her over to the table in the dining room where he'd set everything out ready for them to have their meal.

"Here you are, my lady," he said as he held out a chair for her. "Come and partake of my culinary skills."

"But where did all of this come from?" Mackenzie wanted to know. "When did you do all of this?"

Dean tapped the side of his nose in a conspiratorial manner but would say nothing.

Mackenzie didn't care. She was delighted. He'd thought of everything. Sitting on her plate, Mackenzie spied a red rose. It looked so beautiful. She thought of the symbolic meaning for red roses and wondered if Dean was again, in this small way, affirming his love for her.

"Dean, this is beautiful, so perfect. Where did you get a rose at such short notice?" she wanted to know as she looked across at him.

"A gentleman doesn't divulge his secrets to the woman he loves, but," he said lightly, "just this once, I'll be a cad and tell you. Let me just say that Mrs. Jones, on the other side of my place, now has a garden that is missing one red rose. I don't think she'd have denied you its beauty had she known its final destination."

Mackenzie laughed up at him, totally caught up in the magic of the moment. He was being so gallant, so wonderful, that she forgot about her former fears.

"Hang on," he told her, going into the kitchen where Mackenzie heard the flare of a match being struck and then he was back carrying two candles which were burning brightly in paper cups, "This adds to the atmosphere. Of course, it would help if it was dark outside, but I guess we can't have everything." He stood back to observe his handiwork, and completely satisfied, he sat down, telling her to dig in before he was tempted to eat the lot.

They had a lovely meal that was filled with laughter and merrymaking. Dean had her in stitches, regaling her with stories about his former position. For her part, she had a tale or two that amused him regarding some of her former students and the antics that they'd employ to get out of work.

By mutual consent, they stayed clear of any conversation that would take away the lighthearted mood that had been established between them. They both knew that later would be soon enough to sort through the emotional upheaval that had kept them apart for so long.

All too soon, the meal was finished, Dean stood up, coming around to her. He held out his hand to her, and Mackenzie felt not the slightest bit of hesitation in putting her hand into his.

"Let's go and sit down. I'll clean up later," he told her casually as he led her out into the other room. Dusk had started to settle, and the room was starting to fill with shadows.

Mackenzie commented wryly, "Not only can he cook, but he cleans as well. Just what have I got here?"

"I don't know. Just what you have got here?" he mocked her, smiling down into her upturned face.

"Someone very special, I'm sure," she told him softly as she gazed up into his huge, brown eyes. Tentatively, she caressed the side of his face, loving the feel of his freshly shaven skin beneath her gently probing fingertips. Her fingers lingered over the small mole on the left side of his face before moving on to the firmness of his lips. She traversed the line of his jaw until her fingers had slowly travelled from one side of his face to the other. His ears were investigated with gentle intensity as she sought to familiarise herself with the man who stood patiently before her.

His hair had fallen across his forehead yet again, and she gently pushed the rebellious dark blonde locks back into place, only to find that as soon as she released her hand, they fell back down into natural disarray.

Dean asked her slowly as he smiled down at her, "Do you think you'll be able to find me in a dark room now?"

"Absolutely," she told him finally. "I have been a bit of a bitch, haven't I? It sounds silly to say it out loud, but I was scared of you, of the feelings I was starting to have towards you."

"Of me?" he exclaimed, examining Mackenzie's upturned face.

There was a slight catch in her voice as she carefully tried to explain. "It's kind of hard to put into words, but, well, you're the first man I've really been interested in since Steve died. He was the last man I was intimate with if you get my meaning." She saw Dean's eyebrows creep up towards his hairline, but she continued, knowing she had to finish what she was about to say while she still had the nerve to do so. "That's over three years, Dean. I mean, what if I don't satisfy you?"

Dean shook his head in disbelief, gently grabbing Mackenzie by the shoulders. This was the last thing he'd expected to hear. Not the part about Mackenzie's celibacy, although it rocked him to hear that she hadn't been with a man since the death of her husband, but to think that she was upset about not pleasing him.

"Mackenzie . . . I'm speechless." Dean searched for an appropriate answer, wanting her to know that although he burned to make love to her, he saw their relationship as being so very much more. "Honey, I want so much for the two of us to make love, but more than that, I want us to be friends first. I'm sure that one will follow the other if we respect each other's wishes and well . . . hell, I don't know. But I can tell you right now, you will never be a disappointment to me,

Mackenzie Phillips. Anyway, haven't you heard? Making love is like riding a bike, once you learn, you never forget."

Mackenzie had to smile at the analogy Dean had used. Of course, she'd heard this, but it didn't belay her fears, and she told him so, adding impishly, as an afterthought, "You know, it's funny, but I could never get the hang of riding a bike as a child. I was one of those awkward kids who kept falling off."

"Is that so?" he answered drolly. "You just didn't have the right teacher. I was excellent at riding bikes. Remind me to show you one day."

"You know," he continued softly, "there's one way I could set your mind at ease." He was gazing down at her, looking intently into her brown eyes before he let his gaze wander lovingly over her face. His hands slid slowly down her back, gently caressing her, until they rested lightly on the back of her waist with seemingly remarkable nonchalance. Mackenzie looked steadily up at him, trying to control the havoc his touch wrought on her as her stomach turned upside down in awaited anticipation.

"I . . . um . . ." She couldn't think of one coherent thing to say, not with his hands moving slowly over her trembling body. She felt like she was drowning in his big brown eyes which seemed to hold her captive so easily. She hoped she wasn't making an utter fool of herself, but for the life of her, she couldn't snap out of it. Her own brown eyes reluctantly left the deep chocolate pools that seemed to be swallowing her to rest briefly on the full sensuous lips that were now slightly parted in a half-knowing smile as he became aware of the effect he was starting to have on her.

A small, swift pulse had started to throb at the base of his neck, which gave testimony to the fact that he wasn't as immune to Mackenzie's charms as he would have her think.

"I . . . um . . . what?" he teased as he deliberately took a step backwards, putting a small chasm of space between them. His dark brows lifted suggestively as he waited for an answer.

Mackenzie ran her tongue nervously over her lips. She felt powerless to stop him, or could it be that deep down, she really didn't want to?

"Well?" he insisted as he reached out a hand towards her nubile body. His fingers fleetingly caressed one of her breasts, which brought an instant response to her heated body. She felt her nub instantly harden under his gentle touch.

Mackenzie was being mesmerised by him as he again moved closer to her. He buried his head into her neck and began to lay a succession of light kisses along the base of her neck before plunging his mouth slowly into the cleft of her breasts to make his way over to the centre of her left breast, where he gently nibbled at her through the light fabric of the blouse she was wearing.

After the initial shock, which hit her like a ton of bricks, Mackenzie gave in to the extravagant sensations that had started to pulsate throughout her body. She arched herself against him, throwing her head back, greedily willing him to continue on his conquest of her body.

"Oh my god, Mackenzie, what you do to me?" he whispered into her ear, barely in control of his own emotions. He brought his lips down against hers in a lingering kiss that left her raw with wanting him.

"Prove it," Mackenzie moaned provocatively, hardly aware of what she was doing much less what she was saying.

Dean pulled his lips back from hers, momentarily stunned by the urgent appeal in her voice. He looked vaguely into her eyes, noticing a glazed look which he was sure she'd be able to see mirrored in his own. He was saved from giving a reply as Mackenzie guided his lips back to her own. She savoured the maleness of him as he strove to pull her even closer to his now throbbing body. He burned for her with an urgency that left him breathless.

"Well, now we've gone and done it," Dean told Mackenzie as he nuzzled the soft contours of her neck. She was nestled into his shoulder. She seemed to round off the hard contours of his body with her softness.

"In more ways than one," Mackenzie agreed, laughing at the silly expression that Dean threw at her.

"There's no going back now. You realise that, don't you?" he continued, interjecting each word with featherlike kisses. "I thought I was immune to all of this . . . this," Dean faltered, trying to find the appropriate word for the situation in which he found himself. His eyes travelled around the room, taking everything in at a slow glance before he brought his gaze back to rest lovingly on the woman who lay contentedly at his side.

Mackenzie lifted her weight up onto one elbow. "This . . . this," she prompted casually, delighting in being able to return some of the deliberate jibes he'd thrown at her earlier.

She started to run her fingers through his hair, loving the way the unresisting strands glided so easily through her open grasp. Dean lay unmoving beneath her ministrations, letting her manipulate the moment as she saw fit. For now, she was content only to touch him, to learn more about his body. She noticed he had two horizontal grooves etched into his brow as he watched her weave her magic over him.

She bent over him to slowly kiss away any vestiges of concern that might remain from his noble brow. She could taste him. The salt had formed on his skin after their passionate interlude; it was a tangy reminder that they had consummated their desire for each other. Her breasts feathered softly across his chest, causing him to shudder slightly from the erotic contact. It excited her to know that she had the power to push him beyond the everyday boundaries of his normal existence, that he'd wanted her with an all-consuming passion that couldn't be sated, except by the joining together of their two bodies.

The tip of her tongue explored the ridges running across his forehead; she probed gently, investigating the contours that met her inquiring mouth. This simple act ignited the yearning passion within her as once again, her heated body began to ache for him. She showered his face with kisses while simultaneously caressing him with hands that trembled slightly from the arousing hunger for him that was steadily building in and around her. Her fevered brain registered Dean's laboured breathing, letting her know that he too was feeling the magic of the moment. She called out his name which left her lips as a whimpered moan.

Heat coursed throughout her as Dean reached for her, caressing her breasts so that before very long, she was writhing beneath his manipulative touch. He ran his free hand down the length of her stomach, his fingertips barely touching the delicate area below her navel, but it was enough to send her into a frenzy of excitement that nearly sent her over the top of her passion glazed threshold. She clung to him, desperately willing him with her eyes not to stop this delicious sensation that had taken complete control of her eager body.

By mutual consent, Mackenzie covered his glistening body with her own, hearing as if from far away, his sharp intake of breath as they became one, after which her emotions ran totally berserk as she wantonly gave herself up to the exquisite, sensuous festival that had started a rampant raging through her veins. She was like a forest that had been through a long drought; her body was like the dry bracken that was strewn on the forest floor and was now being consumed at a deadly rate by an all-consuming, raging, white-hot passion that left her totally mindless. Riotous colours exploded in her brain as her body responded to his sensual touch. He played her like a finely tuned instrument which had been left for far too long on the shelf.

CHAPTER FIVE

"Mackenzie, tell me about him. Steve, I mean. He must have been very special to have captured your heart," Dean whispered as he held her closely within the circle of his arms. He knew before they progressed any further that it would be imperative for both of them to get the subject of Steve out into the open.

At first, Mackenzie didn't answer, making him think that she'd fallen asleep. Then she slowly turned away from him until all he could see was her back. He didn't know if he was being rejected or if she was going to answer his question.

"Mackenzie, don't turn away from me. I'd like to know about him, and I'd like you to be the one to tell me. Does that seem so horrible to you, to talk about your dead husband to someone you've just made love with?" He put his hand lightly onto her shoulder, hoping she'd see the innocence behind his request.

When Mackenzie finally spoke, her voice was muffled and sounded very husky. "It's hard to know where to start. It's still hard to think of him as being dead. I seem to think of him as just being away. I know that's silly and possibly even childish, but it's helped me to cope with his loss. I guess that's why I still talk about him as if he was still here."

Dean had reached that particular conclusion himself. He was pleased to hear Mackenzie admit as much to herself. It meant she was finally ready to let him go and get on with the rest of her life.

"Honey," he coaxed, "turn around, let me look at you. It's not a bad thing to have loved someone that much. If you feel only some of that love for me, we can work it out together. You can love me without betraying your late husband's memory. I'm sure he would have wanted you to fall in love again."

Dean felt her tremble under his touch, realising that his words held an element of truth for her.

"I'm sure you're right. He would have wanted me to be happy. He was very special, Dean," Mackenzie told him as she took a deep breath to steady herself. She turned back to face him and Dean could see how she was trying to keep the tears at bay. Her eyes were covered with a fine mist of tears that shimmered as she tried unsuccessfully to blink them away.

He brought her back into the safety of his arms while he urged her to continue.

"Steve was . . . He . . . I was very young, only eighteen when we met, but I knew instantly that I loved him. I had just started university. Steve was in his third year, but we just seemed to click somehow. It seems silly, but we never fought, at least not over major things. We were married four months later, much to the horror of my family, all of whom said our marriage was doomed to failure." Mackenzie wiped the tears away with the back of a trembling hand. She had such happy memories of her time with Steve. Once she'd started to talk about her past, Mackenzie found she was loath to stop. She told Dean everything. The words seemed to spill out of her as if floodgates had been opened that had been shut for far too long.

"It just didn't seem right to push Steve's memory out of the way, so I could make room for someone I wasn't even sure I liked at the time. I'm so used to talking about him . . . I didn't think. He was a good man, Dean." There was a catch in her voice as once again, Mackenzie brushed back the tears, trying to fight the emotion that had been steadily building up inside of her as past memories threatened to overpower her.

"I can understand that. I did the same thing when we first met. I thought I'd fallen head over heels in love with a married woman. The only way I could deal with being near you was to keep you at a discreet distance, but I was failing miserably. Every time I let my guard down and let myself get close to you, we'd have a row. I didn't know what I was going to do next. I've never been so miserable in my life," Dean announced soberly, tightening his hold on her as he laid his chin on the top of her head.

"Like the other night, at the hotel, on the dance floor," Mackenzie said simply, "and those horrible agricultural science lessons." It all seemed to fit now that she knew the reason behind those decisions.

"Exactly. I wanted to be near you, and I thought I could cope with my feelings. Mackenzie, I'm sorry for those things I said. I was out of my mind with jealousy and frustration. The thought of another man being with you was killing me."

"Shh, I'm the one who should be apologising to you, but I just didn't think. I mean, how was I to know you liked me? I actually thought you hated me. Do you know I've been thinking of accepting the teaching position I was offered a while back."

"What? When? Where?" he wanted to know before telling her, "and you should know, I could never dislike you. I've tried, remember? But I failed miserably. You kept creeping into my heart. I'm afraid you're stuck with me for good."

He continued, worried about the news of a proposed transfer, "Have you heard anything back about this other job? If you do, you'll have to tell them you've changed your mind."

"No, no news as yet," she whispered impishly into his ear, "but I'll let you know as soon as I do, okay?"

"Mackenzie, I'm serious," he told her.

"I know and I will. I promise," she answered, knowing now wasn't the time to joke about something of that nature. Both of them were still harbouring raw emotions that needed to heal, but she also knew that those same emotions were well on the way to a remarkable recovery.

A companionable silence had settled over them as they contemplated the conversation they'd broached earlier. Dean finally broke the reverie by asking, "How do you feel now? Has talking about Steve made the situation better or worse?"

"Much better," Mackenzie announced softly. "You always seem to know the right thing to say. Thank you for being so understanding. A lot of men wouldn't have stayed past the first sign of trouble."

"That's their loss and my gain," Dean told her before continuing, "As long as you know it's me, Dean Ashleigh, who's here with you now. I don't want you to push him out of your memory."

"I know exactly who I have in my bed," Mackenzie told him softly, turning in his arms so that she hovered above him with her mouth only inches away from his. It thrilled her to know that if she was to move just the slightest bit more, her breasts would graze his chest, and their lips would meet.

"Is that a fact?" Dean grinned up at her from where he lay. His hand slowly crept up her back, drawing her down towards him.

Mackenzie's body language spoke for her as she let her lips finally merge with Dean's. She felt his heart pounding beneath her as she was held a willing captive against his masculine chest. She was in no doubt that he'd be able to feel her own heart as it had started a vibrant booming within her chest as her need for him escalated.

Her body surged with unbearable desire as she wantonly gave in to the thrill of having Dean touch her. In one deft movement, he rolled over taking her with him. His tongue was greedily searching as he kissed her with abandon before his lips left her mouth to travel feverishly over her body, blazing a tantalising trail that his hands seemed to follow.

Mackenzie was a quivering mess, gasping with giddy pleasure as Dean took one of her nipples into his mouth, his teeth nipped while his tongue lured the pink nub outwards, away from her excited body.

"Dean. Oh god. Dean, how I want you," Mackenzie gasped into his chest. She half rose off the bed and sank her teeth into him as desire flooded her. She hadn't thought it was possible to want anyone this urgently or to feel so much pleasure from the touch of another human being. She vaguely heard the heavy rasp of Dean's breathing as he fought to control himself, but she didn't have the strength to stop the naked exhilaration that was building up within her.

"Dean, please, please now," she pleaded, almost sobbing, knowing she was going to lose herself and career headlong into a deep well of ecstasy. Her body was spinning out of control, and she was powerless to stop it.

Dean entered her, thrusting himself deeply into her, finding her moist and welcoming. Mackenzie arched her back revelling in the heady sensations that had started to converge around her. Her senses took over as instinctively, she opened up to Dean's thrusting body as he drove himself repeatedly into her. He felt the blood roaring in his ears as his world exploded around him.

Time lost all meaning as their bodies merged. It was only later, as they lay frantically, trying to catch their breath, that their world started to slow down once again.

Dean's voice was ragged as he told Mackenzie, "I love you. Don't ever doubt it." He planted a heart-felt kiss at the base of her neck while still trying to catch his breath.

Still caught up in the euphoria of the moment, Mackenzie could only nod. Her body felt soothed and so very relaxed after their hectic bout of lovemaking. Before finally dropping off to sleep, she remembered taking Dean's hand and holding it between her own before she nestled snugly into the curve of his body. Her hands guided his captive hand to her mouth where she gently kissed him on the fingertips before guiding it down to rest securely between the cleft of her breasts.

Mackenzie awoke to the unaccustomed weight of Dean's arm flung casually across her body. She listened for a few moments to his steady breathing as he lay sleeping. A quick glance at the digital clock told her it was four-thirty in the morning, so there was still ample time to enjoy the firm length of his body as he lay stretched out beside her on her large, brass bed, before he would have to leave her.

Carefully taking hold of his hand, she brought it lovingly to her lips, where she proceeded to kiss each fingertip in turn before gingerly intertwining her fingers with his, then she guided his hand with her own, down over her body so that he was holding her more firmly. Satisfied for the moment with this stolen embrace from him, she drifted back to sleep.

Waking some time later, she found the early morning sunlight was already streaming into the bedroom. Dean was no longer holding her because once asleep, she must have shifted her sleeping position. He was, however, still beside her, although no longer sleeping.

Like herself, Dean had only been awake for a few minutes. Smiling lazily at her, he gallantly tried to stifle a yawn.

"Hello," he offered by way of a good morning greeting before he added, "Did you sleep well?"

"Yes," she admitted. She was somewhat surprised to find that in the cold light of day, she was a trifle embarrassed about having Dean in her bed. Oh, she loved him and didn't have a single regret about their night of love making, but she was at a loss as to how you greeted someone you'd just spent the night with when that man wasn't your husband.

Dean must have picked up on her uncertainty because a slight frown covered his beard-stained face, and he felt compelled to ask, "Do you have any regrets?"

"No," she answered honestly, wanting to put his mind at ease on this matter at least.

He sounded genuinely puzzled as he probed, yet again, "Then what's wrong?"

Finding she couldn't meet his persistent gaze, Mackenzie found a spot on the far wall and concentrated all of her energy onto that one little area.

"Mackenzie?" he was unyielding to the point of being obstinate, letting Mackenzie know she'd have to supply him with an answer.

She took a deep breath to fortify herself before blurting out in a rush, "I'm embarrassed. I don't know what to do next. Do I nonchalantly get out of bed? Do I offer . . . ?"

Her words were cut short by Dean's loud hoot of laughter resounding around the bedroom before he told her in an astonished voice, "That's it? You had me worried there for a minute. In answer to your question, you be yourself, just be your loveable . . . beautiful . . . fascinating . . . bewitching . . . charming . . . wonderful . . . insatiable self." He interspersed each of his words with a kiss before he asked leisurely, "Have I put your mind at ease yet?"

"Completely," she told him without hesitation and was promptly on the receiving end of a prolonged good morning kiss.

"Do you know," she confessed soon afterwards, "I could definitely get used to this particular kind of wake-up call?"

"So, my little prude, do I get breakfast, or are you going to send me home with an empty stomach?"

"I'm not a prude," she told him, bestowing on him a look which she hoped would help her to prove her point.

"Prove it," he told her, smiling across the bed at her. Sparkling lights were dancing in his brown eyes as he waited to see if she'd take him up on his casually thrown out challenge.

Sometime later, he was forced to admit defeat. "Okay . . . you win. You're definitely not a prude." He was still gasping for breath as a low triumphant laugh escaped from Mackenzie's throat before she gave in once again to the euphoria that was starting to claim her body.

She didn't have the energy to move, let alone claim a victory as she was still experiencing the wonderful rapture that had resulted in the merging of their heated bodies. Their legs were still intertwined, but neither one of them made a move to break the intimate contact that kept them together. Mackenzie felt a sense of peace that she was sure she communicated to Dean without a word being spoken between them.

Dean sighed contentedly, and his breath singed her hair as it lay sprawled across his chest, burning her to the very depths of her being. She was his forever. He'd made a formidable conquest without even knowing it.

She lifted languid eyes to him which mirrored the depths of her very soul. Mackenzie was convinced she saw a similar look captured and held in his own brown orbs as he gazed steadily back at her before they were both transported back into peaceful sleep.

"Holy hell! Mackenzie, wake up. Look at the time." Someone was shaking her, much to her chagrin. She didn't want to wake up from the wonderful dream she was sharing with Dean. Dean was . . . Damn it. Dean was shaking her. She opened bleary, brown eyes to look up at him as he sat perched on the side of the bed.

"What's wrong," she mumbled, trying to wake up.

"We've overslept." He grinned down at her. "And some people have to get to work."

Fighting the urge to roll over and let sleep reclaim her, Mackenzie focused her attention on the small digital clock which sat on her bedside table. The numbers indicated that they had indeed overslept. It was nearly nine o'clock in the morning.

With all traces of sleep gone, she sat bolt upright in bed. "Do you have any early morning appointments?" Mackenzie asked, worried now that he was definitely going to be late.

"Thankfully, no," he told her as he pulled on the clothes he'd worn the night before. They were crumpled and creased, showing definite signs of the haste in which they'd been discarded the night before.

"You know, the school has probably been trying to phone you. What will you tell them?" she was a bit apprehensive about telling the world of her budding relationship with Dean at this early stage.

It had only been one night. It was, after all, very new and fragile. She didn't think she was ready for all of the comments that would be conveyed to her about life and love, and in particular, Dean.

He arched his eyebrows as he looked down at her from where he stood beside the bed. He could sense the hesitation lurking behind her luminous brown eyes and realised that she'd rather they kept their relationship to themselves for the time being.

"Oh, I'll think of something," he confided to her. "I've been having trouble with the battery in my car for a while now, so perhaps I can let everyone think it finally gave up the ghost."

"Thank you, Dean," Mackenzie said meekly. It meant a lot to her that he understood how she was feeling.

"Don't mention it," he said mockingly as he brought his lips down to capture hers in a fleeting kiss.

He was heading out of the bedroom door when Mackenzie asked him uncertainly, "Dean, am I going to see you later?"

He came back into the bedroom and sat down on the side of the bed next to her. "Yes, my paranoid little poppet, you are definitely going to see me this afternoon and the afternoon after that and the one after that and so on. Understand this, Mackenzie Phillips, I love you and I want to be with you, hopefully, for the rest of our lives. Does that answer your question?"

Nodding her understanding, Mackenzie finally let him go. He was involved in a race against time, having yet to go home to shower, shave, and change into more suitable clothing befitting of a high school deputy principal.

The next day, Mackenzie returned to her duties at school, no longer seeing any reason for her to take the extra days off as she'd intended. Her self-imposed crisis had resolved itself when her relationship with Dean, which she hoped would continue to grow, had veered off in a new direction.

She was faced with a barrage of questions from her colleagues as to why she'd been away, but she was able to fob everyone off by telling them that she'd been the unwilling victim of a certain teacher's lack of ability to mind his own business where her private life was concerned.

Brian, the teacher in question, looked at her sheepishly from across the staffroom. "I'm sorry, Mac, truly, I am," he told her truthfully. "I was only trying to help out a friend, one whom I thought needed cheering up rather desperately."

Mackenzie was enjoying the situation immensely as she answered enthusiastically, "Cheering up, yes, but to mount a full-scale attack on my nervous system by plying me with all of that alcohol, that was something else." She walked over to him and said casually, "Do you have any idea of how sick I was on Saturday? I felt like my head was going to explode."

Brian had the grace to look crestfallen before promising that he would never again spike another drink as long as he lived, much to the general laughter of everyone in the staffroom, most of whom had been on the receiving end of one of Brian's practical jokes.

The incessant clanging of the lineup bell put an end to any more queries for the moment, but Mackenzie realised that her day probably held greetings from well-wishers wanting to know about her present state of health.

Handling questions of this calibre wouldn't be difficult, and Mackenzie didn't foresee any problems in providing reasonable answers as to her whereabouts since the previous Friday night, when she'd blindly stumbled off the dance floor in a valiant bid to make Dean listen to her.

That horrible night seemed so long ago, Mackenzie thought, marvelling at how much had transpired in her life as a direct result of the circumstances surrounding her forced confrontation with Dean.

Thinking of him brought a small secret smile to her lips as she recalled with precise clarity the time they'd spent together over the course of the last few days.

Everyone was readying themselves for the day ahead. In an effort to vindicate himself of any wrong doing, Brian said to everyone in general before the staffroom was vacated, "Anyway, correct me if I'm wrong, but Mackenzie does seem to be revitallised after her time off. She's positively glowing, just look at her." All eyes in the staffroom centered on Mackenzie, making her feel acutely embarrassed about her state of well-being. To make matters worse, she could feel a telltale flush creeping up from her neck, covering her face with a bright crimson hue.

"See, what did I tell you?" Brian was like a dog with a bone. He wasn't about to let the matter rest when there was obviously a chance to extricate himself from the role of school villain.

Thinking quickly, Mackenzie said, "Of course I'm embarrassed, you silly old goat. Who wouldn't be under the circumstances? Now get going, or you'll be late for your class. Your students will be thinking they have a free period."

Running into Dean later in the day, Mackenzie quickly smothered the joyful look that transformed her face from one of apt concentration to that of ardent anticipation. He didn't break his stride or stop to communicate, taking their chance meeting entirely in his stride, but he threw Mackenzie's caution to the wind when he winked outrageously at her while mouthing the words "I love you" before he continued casually on his way.

Their unscheduled meeting had Mackenzie's heart pounding against her ribs, and his silent vow which professed his love for her was very nearly her undoing. She was sorely tempted to follow him, to wreak havoc on her self-imposed composure by screaming from the roof tops that she loved Dean Ashleigh with every fibre of her being, that she belonged to him in body, heart, soul, and mind.

Knowing it was only a matter of time before their relationship would become public knowledge, Mackenzie was still reluctant to confess her love for Dean in front of an audience. She pondered long and hard on the various reasons behind her decision and was continually drawn to the constant conclusion that their relationship, although firm and flourishing, had a very shaky beginning, one which was still very fresh in her mind.

She also realised that Dean, being the kind of man he was, wouldn't want to have a relationship that was constantly carried on behind closed doors. She instinctively knew that he would eventually want everyone to know about their association and that they'd moved on from being mere friends to something of a more serious nature. He would only go along with her request for secrecy for so long before he too started to demand answers as to why they were compelled to keep their love in the dark, away from the people who knew them.

The holidays were nearly upon them. Two glorious weeks of doing nothing but getting to know each other as companions and lovers. Perhaps after this period of time, Mackenzie would be comfortable telling her fellow workers and friends that she'd inexplicably fallen head over heels in love with Dean.

Mackenzie was under no illusions that as soon as Dean had had enough of the continued cloak-and-dagger routine that she was playing, he'd soon put a stop to it, ending the charade she was wanting to play with her co-workers; but for some reason that she couldn't entirely determine herself, it was important to her that they had their privacy at least for now.

"There's still so much we don't know about each other," Mackenzie said idly one afternoon as they shared a cup of coffee while sitting at his kitchen table. She'd been looking at the enormous volume of books which completely filled a very large bookshelf standing in the corner of the lounge room. The titles were many and varied, giving an indication that he was very well read on any number of subjects.

"I like chocolate ice-cream," he tossed at her sincerely, looking deeply into her own chocolate eyes as he related this piece of news.

"Is that so?" she answered, valiantly trying to keep the smirk from her delicate features.

He was nodding his head, affirming his claim. Mackenzie refused to let herself become flustered by his light-hearted banter. Instead, she carried on with the charade, adding small tidbits of near useless information herself. They carried on until each had exhausted most of the trivial knowledge about themselves that they could dredge up from the distant memories of childhood.

"But," Dean told Mackenzie casually when it was again his turn to enlighten her with a useless bit of background data, "all of that stuff takes a distant second place when it comes to you, even the chocolate ice cream."

The grin he sent her across the table was almost her undoing. He looked like a little boy who had just told someone his innermost, most precious secret. Mackenzie's skin turned into a series of goose bumps as she took in the enormity of what he was telling her. She was sure her response was openly mirrored in her eyes for him to see. She was on the verge of telling him so when the incessant ringing of the telephone interrupted their personal respite.

"Saved by the bell," she advised him and was relieved to know that he clearly understood her implied meaning because as he rose purposely from his chair, he placed a quick kiss on to her soft lips, which spoke volumes about his current feelings.

"Won't be long," he informed her as he headed for the telephone. "You can tell me later what you were going to say, okay?"

As he listened to the voice on the other end of the phone, his demeanour suddenly changed from the easy going man who had been her companion to that of an astute stranger who became very businesslike and shrewd.

His answers were clipped and short as he held the telephone to his ear. His back was to Mackenzie, so she couldn't see his features as he spoke, but she was certain they'd match his stance which had become rigid and unrelenting.

Rejoining her a few minutes later, although he was smiling, Mackenzie could see that the gaiety didn't reach his eyes. A veil had been pulled firmly into place. She was at a loss as to the conversation that had taken place, and Dean didn't seem to want to vouchsafe any information regarding the identity of his caller.

"Bad timing," she offered as a way of breaking the silence that was threatening to envelop them. She could see that the call had clearly upset him; also, he seemed reluctant to talk about it to her.

"You could say that," he told her, which only served to make Mackenzie more confused. Where was the trust they'd promised to share with each other? Had he only been paying lip service when he'd spoken about trust and honesty? His next words to her seemed to pave the way for Mackenzie's doubts to fester.

"Mackenzie," he said, almost reluctantly. "I have to go out. Something has come up which I should really look into." His voice, although calm, brooked no argument; and Mackenzie found herself scrambling to her feet in an effort to do as he was silently requesting of her and leave as soon as possible.

Finding she couldn't leave without first asking if everything was alright, she was given a brief nod, which did nothing to quieten the growing sense of concern that was starting to build up within her.

Thoroughly confused, Mackenzie headed for the door. Just when she thought their relationship was starting to make headway, it seemed they'd hit a snag. She had to remind herself that they weren't officially a couple. If he felt the need to with-hold information of a personal nature, then she really didn't have the right to protest, but that didn't mean that she had to stop caring or worrying about whatever was causing the gleam to be absent from his eyes.

It all came back to the question of trust, and come what may, she was determined to trust him. It was of paramount importance after the shaky beginning their growing relationship had suffered.

"Will I see you later?" she had to force the words out, for her mouth had gone very dry. She found his answer was extremely important to her.

"Maybe not tonight," he answered frankly, making Mackenzie's hopes of a shared evening plummet into the depths of despair.

Seeing her obvious disappointment, Dean smiled, trying to ease the sudden tension which he could see building up in Mackenzie's manner. His head tilted slightly as he regarded her standing rigidly in front of him.

"Hey, what's this?" he wanted to know, placing a long finger under Mackenzie's chin as he forced her to look up at him.

"Nothing," she lied, trying to keep the disappointment out of her voice. It wouldn't do for them to argue over a figment of her imagination, for it instantly occurred to her that she was jealous, but of whom, that was the one missing link to this whole sorry tale.

"Mackenzie," he said coaxingly as if he was talking to one of his students. "Talk to me. Where do you think I'm going?"

Mackenzie was refusing to look at him; therefore, she missed the expression in his eyes, but she could hear the derision that flowed from his deep voice.

"That's obvious. You're going to meet the person who was on the other end of that telephone call," she threw back at him, hoping he didn't miss the scorn she'd purposely implanted in her dulcet tones.

"Ouch." He winced. "If I had the time, I'd tell you exactly what I think of women who throw jealous tantrums every time their man is called away from their side."

"I'm not jealous," Mackenzie tossed back at him, knowing the words that rolled so easily off her tongue to be untruths of the highest degree; but at the same time, she was thrilled to hear him say that he was her man. It gave her hope for their future together.

Skepticism danced in Dean's eyes as he gazed down at her.

"Ah-uh, although a little bit of jealousy is nice from time to time, it makes a man feel appreciated, but don't overdo it, will you?" His eyes were deep, dark pools of merriment as he reached for her, drawing her into his rich embrace. He rested his chin on the top of her head as he told her softly, "I'm sorry if I sounded distant before, but this is something I have to do, some business I have to clear up. You'll just have to trust me like I trust you."

Mackenzie trembled in Dean's embrace, trying valiantly to believe in him and their love.

"Okay," she told him timidly, willing herself to be strong. She felt a sting of shame at the way her thoughts had led her, but they had been too strong to suppress. She vowed to try harder in the future. It was incredible; she was learning things about her character that she hadn't known she possessed. Was it possible that she was capable of turning into a screeching shrew if she was slighted in love? The thought brought a slight smile to her lips, and she actually chuckled at the picture her mind presented to her.

"Dean," she asked him as he studied her face suspiciously, "kiss me."

Dean's eyebrows shot up, and he fixed his deep, brown eyes on her face, trying to fathom out the reasoning behind her sudden request to be kissed.

"Please," she whispered, all traces of laughter wiped from her face.

Lowering his lips to hers as he'd been bidden, Dean was surprised at the intensity of Mackenzie's embrace as she kissed him with a passion that belied all of her hasty thoughts where he was concerned. They clung to each other, enveloped in a golden hue of passion which threatened to overcome them. Dean groaned as he held Mackenzie close to his fevered body, loving the way she seemed to mold herself to his long, hard length.

He shuddered as he stepped back, breaking the contact between them. If he didn't leave now, he was in grave danger of taking Mackenzie into his arms and making love to her here and now.

"Mackenzie," he told her, unsteadily. "I have to go. Please, my love, let me go."

It filled Mackenzie with a sense of longing to know that she was the reason for Dean's plea. She loved him with an all-consuming passion that threatened to extinguish any coherent thought she might have on the subject.

Later that night, she heard Dean's car pull into the driveway of his home, and although her lights were on, he made no attempt to make contact with her.

The last day of school rolled around, and Mackenzie found she was more than ready for the two-week break, which stretched temptingly ahead of her. Her plans to spend her vacation with Dean had been put on hold, mainly due to the fact that he hadn't challenged her about her holiday plans when he'd been told about her proposed trip. She'd made arrangements to visit her parents and could see no reason to make any changes to her agenda at this stage. Having made this decision, Mackenzie couldn't see any reason which would delay her leaving. He'd been a little elusive since that mysterious phone call from the other evening.

She'd seen little of Dean during the last few days, so she didn't know if he had any travel plans of his own. Checking her pigeon hole Friday afternoon, Mackenzie saw she had a hastily scribbled note from him, asking her if she could spare a minute to see him before she left for home. The note was very impersonal and cold to Mackenzie's way of thinking, and it was with a sense of foreboding that she dragged her unwilling feet down to his office. She was granted a reprieve when she was told that Dean had been called away on urgent business.

"He said to tell you he'd get in touch with you, Mackenzie," the office girl told her when she asked if she knew what the meeting was about. She was giving Mackenzie a curious stare, trying to fathom out in her mind just what was going on between them.

The next best thing, Mackenzie thought, would be for her to visit Dean's home in an effort to find out what it was he wanted to tell her. This filled her with a delicious tingling as she hadn't had the chance to touch him in days.

Upon arrival, her knock wasn't answered nor did he answer when she called out to him. She gingerly opened the door and was relieved to hear the shower running. Walking up the hallway, Mackenzie knocked on the bathroom door, making her presence known to him.

"Hey, in there, how long are you going to be? I've been waiting out here for ages," she said to the closed door.

She was relieved to hear his deep voice as he told her in muffled tones, "Holy hell, you scared the life out of me. Okay, I won't be long. Make us some coffee, will you? I've got something to tell you."

Dean's cologne pervaded her nostrils as Mackenzie walked through the house. She breathed deeply, loving the image that the spicy fragrance presented to her. One of his shirts was thrown untidily across the back of a chair, and she stooped to pick it up, hugging the fabric close to her body. She could see him standing before her, looking so masculine and virile with his chest muscles rippling as he reached out for her, drawing her into a tight embrace, holding her against the hard length of him.

She ached for him and was sorely tempted to join him in the shower. In fact, she'd actually turned, starting to walk down the hallway that led to her ultimate heart's desire, when the ringing of the telephone halted her in her tracks. *Rotten contraption*, she thought as she veered off her course to answer the call. It could be important, and it would only take a minute, then she could be with her love.

She was on the verge of picking the receiver up when Dean's recorded message filled the room. His voice had a deep resonant sound, making Mackenzie pause to listen, loving the sexy highs and lows that emanated from his throat. She'd been mesmerised by his forceful tones on more than one occasion, especially when he was in the throes of passion. There was a husky vibration that thrilled her to the very depth of her soul.

Mackenzie was stopped dead in her tracks as she became an unwilling, silent listener to the message that was being conveyed onto Dean's answering machine. With each word, she felt him being pulled further away from her as the woman caller recorded her heart wrenching plea for help.

"Dean . . . call me when you can. It's very important. I need to talk to you as soon as possible," the female voice was becoming very distraught. She continued brokenly, "I did as you suggested . . . I took a pregnancy test . . . and . . . and like it or not . . . you're going to be a . . . ," the voice broke again before saying tearfully, "Oh, Dean . . . what am I going to do? Please, Dean, please, phone me. I need your help more than ever."

Mackenzie felt her body turn to stone as the voice on the other end of the line relayed its heartfelt message; she stood, staring at the electrical gadget like it was her mortal enemy. This had to be some sort of a sick joke. She could feel the blood draining away from her face, and her body had started to shake uncontrollably as she took in the enormity of the situation. Her legs felt like they were going to collapse from under her as the reality of the situation hit her with a tremendous force. Dean not only had another lover, but she was pregnant with his child. How could he do this to her and to the other woman who was obviously expecting him to do the right thing and marry her, or so it seemed to Mackenzie?

"Jazz, hi, listen, I'm on my way to pick up my car," Mackenzie marveled at how she was able to keep the hysterics out of her voice as she casually made travel plans over the phone. She felt like screaming out to the world about Dean's betrayal of her, but she knew better than to do this over the phone. When it came to Dean,

Jazz had a misguided sense of loyalty. This time, Mackenzie wasn't going to be badgered into anything that she thought was wrong. Her heart was breaking at the mere thought of him being with another woman. It hurt her to think that all this time she'd been sharing him.

She had to get away, for facing Dean wasn't what she had in mind for herself, given her present state of mind. She could see a pattern forming where he was concerned, but it was one that she was determined to break. Running away wasn't a habit she was used to practicing, but for now it seemed the only reasonable form she could take as a way of preserving her sanity.

Leaving Dean a hurriedly scribbled note, she told him she had the offer of a lift from a fellow teacher who was travelling south for the holiday break. She knew this was a feeble excuse, but time was marching on, and she needed to get away. If she hurried, she could make her way to the shops which were located a few blocks away, ring a taxi which would take her to the bus depot, where hopefully she could board a bus which would take her far away from Dean Ashleigh.

The initial shock of the phone message was starting to wear off, and instead of feeling angry and hurt, Mackenzie was shrouded in a valley of cold misery. She didn't seem to be feeling anything at all. Her mind was numb which suited her just fine. Mackenzie prayed that Dean wouldn't try to follow her when he saw that she had gone.

The words on the answering machine were ringing in her ears, telling her that Dean would be kept busy sorting out some of his other problems over the course of the next few days. She vowed to herself that she wouldn't speak to him if he was to phone her. Her life seemed to be very complicated again all of a sudden, and she found she was longing for the tranquility and peace that had been hers before the arrival of Dean Ashleigh into her life. She might have lived alone, but at least she'd been reasonably happy in her own small world.

"Do you think you're ready to tell me what's been bothering you? You've hardly said a word about Dean since you arrived. You've rambled on about every other subject, bar him. Now while that might fool some people, this is me, your best friend, so out with it. I want to know all of the gory details. In my book, not spilling the beans is tantamount to treason or such like." Jazz was giving Mackenzie a shrewd glance, one that didn't miss the pale, wan face or the fine stress lines that feathered out from her eyes and mouth like tell-tale signposts, which led her to presume that Mackenzie's visit to pick up her car wasn't entirely the whole truth.

"Come on, my friend, out with it. What has that brute of a man been doing now?"

"Dean's not a brute. He's been so wonderful. The past few weeks have been so wonderful." Mackenzie found herself defending him against the allegations that Jazz was piling on his head even though she realised her friend wasn't being serious. Her voice faltered, but she valiantly tried to sound normal, smiling, but failing miserably, so she just shrugged her shoulders instead, afraid of giving in to the tears that were threatening to break down her hard won composure.

"Ah!" Jazz threw at her, starting to smell a rat. "Okay, so he's wonderful. The last few days have been wonderful. Does that include today by any chance?"

Staring across the table at her friend, Mackenzie knew she should answer that particular question. Shrugging matter-of-factly, she said, "Yes, of course." But she couldn't quite meet Jazz's eyes. She started playing with her coffee cup, running her fingers slowly around the thick ceramic rim before taking a deep breath and blurting out, "Actually, no . . . Well . . . no."

"Make up your mind, Mackenzie. I'm starting to get very confused." Jazz was trying to be glib. She could see Mackenzie was fighting her emotions, obviously wanting to talk; but for some reason, she was holding herself back, probably because of loyalty to Dean, which Jazz found to be very sweet.

"Jazz, I don't know what to tell you. My track record with Dean, believing in him, has been lousy. Even you would have to agree with me on that score. I don't know what to think anymore, but when you're presented with concrete facts, what are you supposed to do?"

"What's wrong with me, Jazz? Have I become so dependent on him that I'm willing to take second place where love is concerned?" Mackenzie looked across at Jazz, knowing her friend was also at a loss to explain Dean's erratic behaviour.

"I'm sure there's a logical reason for all of this," Jazz told her. "It doesn't seem right. There's something wrong somewhere. Tell me again what you heard on that darn phone." Jazz found it hard to take in the circumstances surrounding her friend's obvious dilemma. Her relationship with Dean certainly seemed to be fraught with ongoing problems. Could she have been wrong about him after all? Maybe he was a womaniser who liked to chase after other women, but the image of Dean having a string of women on the line just didn't fit the Dean Ashleigh she'd come to know. Surely, a person wasn't able to change so drastically in so short a time. There had to be another explanation, for the man she knew wouldn't profess his love for one woman while he was still seeing someone else. Betrayal wasn't something Dean would be party to, of that much she was certain.

"It seems so stupid. Why don't I just give him up. You know I got that transfer, don't you, if I want it, that is? I've been given a while to make up my mind. Probably because of that darn student and his accusations. I guess it's the department's way of getting me out of the way, I don't know. Anyway, perhaps moving to a district in the back of beyond would solve my problems." Mackenzie was filled with an overwhelming misery that seemed to chill her to her very bones. She didn't see that she had any choice in the matter now; all aspects of the situation had been taken out of her hands. There didn't seem to be any other way out. She'd have to give him up for the sake of the other woman in his life. Given the set of circumstances, she felt sure he'd do the decent thing and marry this person; it was, after all, his child she was carrying.

"Don't you mean running away," Jazz fired at her. She wasn't one for backing down. Mackenzie should have remembered. "Now, let's get back to the matter at hand. Tell me what you heard. Maybe you misinterpreted the message. There could be a perfectly logical explanation to explain all of this. I'd bet my bottom dollar that he loves you."

Mackenzie was exasperated. She knew she'd have to go over all of the heart-wrenching details again in order for Jazz to begin piecing together the puzzle that surrounded Dean's bizarre phone message.

"Jazz, I don't want to go through this again. For god's sake, just let me get over him. Damn, how do I get myself into these situations?" Mackenzie bemoaned. She felt miserable; all she wanted to do was to sink her weary bones into a nice warm bath and then collapse into a nice comfortable bed.

"You fell in love! There's no puzzle there," Jazz told her bluntly. She was unremitting as she eyed Mackenzie from across the kitchen table, relenting a bit when she saw her friend's eyes were starting to fill with unshed tears. She reached across the table consolingly and placed a comforting hand over both of Mackenzie's as she clasped her hands together in front of her, clearly feeling the effects of the emotional battle she was waging against herself. Jazz urged her to start, knowing she needed to lift this particular emotional beast from her shoulders before she could start to settle down and heal the tremendous rift that lay yawning between herself and Dean.

"Come on, you'll feel much better once you've talked it out. Also, you might recall something, some small fact, anything, that might be the key to unravelling this awful mess. Anyway, where would you find such a willing listener at this time of night? Honestly, you do have a knack of getting upset at the darndest times, my friend."

Mackenzie knew there wasn't going to be an easy way out. Jazz was adamant, but most of all, Mackenzie knew she was right. She did need to talk, and Jazz had always been there for her in the past. They were more like sisters than best friends, with Mackenzie using her as an emotional springboard for all of her ideas and most of her problems.

"Did I fall in love, Jazz, or do I just think its love? This feeling, whatever it is, just doesn't seem to fit into any of the usual categories that people in love usually follow. Where's the trust, the respect? I thought we had both of those things going for us, but now I just don't know. With Steve, it was so different. We were perfect together. It was as though we knew what the other was thinking. Now I feel as if I'm trapped in the eye of a cyclone, and there's no way out except through some very rough weather. I don't know if I want to go that way. Maybe it's just lust for both of us."

"Love is a funny thing, but your worst problem is that you keep comparing Dean with Steve. That's a big mistake. Steve was your security blanket. He was your buffer against the rest of the world, keeping you safe, and then he was taken away from you. Also, you were no more than an infant when you married him. Now you're a woman with a woman's feelings. Things change, Mackenzie. You've changed. You had to, to survive. I don't think you could go back to Steve now after knowing Dean. You've grown too much . . . Don't look at me like that. You know I'm right. I'm not knocking Steve or his memory. What you had with him was wonderful, but now he's gone. The only trouble is you won't let go. For years, you've buried yourself in a grave alongside a dead man. Then along comes a man who knocks you off your feet, and you're scared stiff. Your life has been moving very fast, but I'm sure everything will work out as it should."

Mackenzie didn't have the heart to tell Jazz that she was wrong. Unchecked tears were spilling down her cheeks as she tried to find the appropriate words which would explain exactly how she was feeling, but she was unable to speak due to the lump that had formed in her throat. Try as she might, she was unable to stop the flow of tears, and finally giving up in defeat, she laid her weary head in her hands and wept. She cried for Steve, realising she hadn't really said good-bye to him in her heart. She cried for Dean and their love, wondering if she'd really given it the nurturing a new love needed in order to grow and survive, but mostly, she cried for herself. She felt miserable. It had been a long time since she'd afforded herself the luxury of cleansing tears that served to wash away all of the past pain from her heart. She loved Dean, of that she was certain. She loved everything that went into making him the man he was. The way he made her laugh at the corny jokes he sometimes told her. The way he made her feel so very special as if nothing but her ultimate happiness mattered to him, especially when he held her in his arms after they'd made love. Even the quiet times when they sat together or the times when they'd converse on any number of subjects. He was always with her because she carried him in her heart, and she knew she always would. She just wasn't sure if she'd captured the special place which was in Dean's heart. She needed to know if he really loved her, or was he only marking time while he made up his mind about whom he should choose? The thought of sharing him with someone else tore at her heart strings. What action was she supposed to take? Did she pretend she wasn't aware that he was involved with another woman, or did she confront him with the news in the hope that he would tell her the truth? Mackenzie realised sadly that she knew the answer to that particular question already. She had too much respect for herself to allow herself to play second fiddle to Dean's other lover. Regardless of how much ending their brief relationship would hurt her, there didn't seem to be any other course of action for her to take.

"Feeling better now?" Jazz wanted to know as she handed her another cup of coffee. These emotions had been steadily building, adding to her feelings of misery over the last few hours. Jazz knew she was feeling fragile and unsure of herself, afraid of making a move, lest it be in the wrong direction.

"Much. You had to come to the rescue yet again though, hey." Mackenzie smiled weakly as she sipped her coffee from a mug which ironically had splashed across its side, "Love will find a way if you let it" in big, bold, red letters. She added contritely, "I'm sorry to burden you with all of my problems. How do you put up with me?"

"I manage," Jazz smiled impishly then continued, throwing her friend a knowing look, "anyway, where else would I get to hear such things? It makes my dull life so very interesting, don't you know?"

Laughing despite herself, Mackenzie knew she'd been right to come here. Jazz always seemed to know what to do, having a special knack of making a person face their problems head on.

Studying Mackenzie's face, Jazz could see that some of the natural colour had returned to transfuse a healthier tan, but she still didn't look anything like her old self. Considering her next words carefully, she said, "You know you have to confront Dean with all of this, don't you? You can't keep running away." She scratched her head as she searched for the appropriate words to say. "I just can't see him in this role, Mackenzie. If this other woman is pregnant and the child is his, then I suspect they had a relationship prior to the two of you meeting."

Mackenzie had come to the same conclusion. "Perhaps, but where does that leave me, still out in the cold as far as I can see. I know I have to face him, but what am I going to say?" Mackenzie's voice was a hoarse whisper as she tried unsuccessfully to gain some semblance of control over her ragged emotions. Swallowing convulsively, she looked into the eyes of her friend, hoping she'd be able to find some plausible answers in their blue depths.

Shrugging her slim shoulders, Jazz knew Mackenzie wasn't going to like what she was about to hear. "I think perhaps you might have been a bit impulsive. You should have stayed and talked this problem out." Seeing the hurt expression settle onto Mackenzie's face didn't lesson the fact that these things had to be said. "Damn it, Mackenzie, don't look at me like that. Just let me finish. If it turns out that I'm wrong, you can throw it up to me for the rest of our lives. Dean loves you. His love for you shines out of him like a beacon, but you're the only one who can't see it." She tried to make Mackenzie understand. "You caused the rift in the relationship, so it's up to you to mend it." She was through with sugar coating her comments, knowing it was time for her friend to grow up and accept responsibility for her life. She needed to take a long hard look at herself and at the direction her life was heading.

Deliberately taking her time to drive home, Mackenzie's stomach was a mass of nerves by the time she finally drove into her driveway. She'd turned the conversation she'd have with Dean over in her mind until she felt she knew exactly what she'd say, but now that the moment had arrived, every last word had been magically wiped from her memory, leaving her mind as clear as a slate that had been wiped clean by the hands of fate.

Some of Jazz's words of the night before came back to haunt her. Their discussion had become very heated, with Mackenzie being rebuked for her stupidity in leaving without giving Dean a chance to vindicate himself.

"Do you know how much your actions have probably hurt him?" Jazz had rounded on her savagely. She was past caring about how Mackenzie felt and had gone on, not heeding her friends down-trodden demeanour. "It's not only a woman's prerogative to be deeply hurt, you know, and this time, I think you've excelled yourself beyond even my worst expectations of you. For god's sake, Mackenzie, grow up, become a woman before it's too late to even try." Upon delivering this blunt piece of advice, Jazz had turned abruptly on her heel and stormed out of the room, leaving Mackenzie staring after her completely dumbfounded. After this, they'd talked well into the night, discussing different components of Mackenzie's life. Jazz had apologised for her radical outburst but had been told by Mackenzie that she'd needed to hear these things in order to come to her senses.

Now she was on the verge of facing Dean, she was afraid she'd ruined any chance of happiness with him. She wanted so badly to see him, to get this awful business over with. She was sure her hasty flight would have serious repercussions that she was going to have to deal with. *Fate could be so cruel sometimes*, she thought as she fumbled with the key to her front door. Her hands were trembling so badly, the key slipped from her fingers. Dejectedly, she placed her head against the door momentarily allowing herself a moment of self-pity in which time she tried to pull herself together, but she failed miserably. She felt physically sick as she contemplated the coming confrontation with Dean that lay before her.

Her house smelt stale as she walked through the empty rooms that only days ago had been filled with the sounds of laughter and love. Her mind conjured up images of those happier times when she'd been held in Dean's passionate embrace, crying out with sheer delight as her desires had been fulfilled.

"Please, God," she prayed as warm tears scalded her eyes, "don't let it be too late for us. I love him."

Wanting to get this awful mess cleared up, Mackenzie didn't bother to freshen up but immediately set out for Dean's home where she could see a single light burning, which meant that he was home. Added to this, his car was parked haphazardly in the driveway. She wondered if he'd heard her drive in as she made her way silently across the stretch of lawn which separated their two houses.

Almost against her will, Mackenzie's eyes took in the large, old poinciana tree which stood just inside the boundary of Dean's yard. Had it only been a few nights ago that they had lain beneath its sweeping branches, looking up at the starlit sky above them? They had found they had another common interest in astronomy and had been trying to distinguish some of the constellations that can be seen in the southern hemisphere. Mackenzie's mouth formed a reluctant smile as she remembered their passionate embraces which had been cut short by the uncaring nip of a bull ant biting her ungallantly on the behind. She'd yelped in outraged pain which, in turn, had caused Dean to think he'd hurt her. Her body burned with suppressed passion as she recalled how he'd ministered to the bite, using his lips to caress the stinging area of her body, thus taking away the sharp pain and replacing it with a wanting so intense she'd almost wished the pain back.

Slowly turning away from the tree, Mackenzie thought she'd be able to leave the memories behind; but she sadly realised that whatever the outcome of tonight's encounter with Dean, she would always remember every second of their time spent together.

Deliberately taking a deep breath, hoping to calm herself, Mackenzie walked up the few steps that would take her to Dean's front door, which was closed against her. Taking this to be a bad omen for their love, she hesitated before finding the courage to knock lightly. The air around her was filled with silence which was strange for usually Dean had music playing. They enjoyed the same taste in music and, on more than one occasion, had danced to the sounds of rock and roll, ballads, and even country, laughing into each other's faces as they found yet another link to add to the chain which was bringing them closer together.

On the verge of leaving because of the quietness behind the closed door, Mackenzie's movement was arrested when she finally heard footsteps coming down the hallway from the back of the house. Her heart was in her mouth as she nervously waited for him to open the door. She wondered if he would invite her inside, or would she have to deliver her speech here in the doorway like an unwanted, unwelcome stranger?

When the door finally opened, the face that greeted her was definitely haggard, and Mackenzie could see the pain lurking in the deep shadows which seemed to be etched into Dean's face. He really did look terrible. It was apparent that he'd forgone his daily shave, having the start of a healthy growth of hair covering his face and neck. His hair was spiked as if he had been running his fingers constantly through the silky strands. The parts of his face which were free of hair looked pale in contrast to his normal tan. If Mackenzie didn't know better, she would have said that he wasn't well.

Wanting nothing more than to run into his arms to let herself be held in his strong masculine embrace was the force that kept her rooted to the spot, regardless of the fact that his stance showed that he'd forbid any such action on her part.

He was bare-chested, wearing only a pair of blue jeans which were slung low over his slim hips, showing his small compact navel while caressing his long legs almost lovingly. Running her tongue over her lips, Mackenzie feasted her eyes on the absolute banquet that was being presented to her. She couldn't control the tingle of pleasure that passed through her, even though the man who stood before her bore not the slightest resemblance to the man she loved.

Momentarily stuck for words, Mackenzie could only stare, and it seemed as if Dean wasn't going to help her out by coming to her rescue with any explanations of his own as to why anyone would leave a message such as the one she'd heard the other day. She wished with all of her heart that she could turn back the clock and have this time over again, being certain that she'd handle herself differently.

"Dean," she began tentatively, her heart aching as she saw him visibly flinch when he heard his name on her lips. He was hurting, but it still remained to be seen if she was the sole reason for his pain, fervently wishing now that she'd stayed to let him explain the contents of the phone message. She remembered that she'd promised to trust him, and she'd broken that trust at the first sign of trouble, but she added silently to herself, *That was before I knew about his other lover.* Perhaps he was only trying to save himself, or perhaps he was looking so anguished because he'd been found out. This would be a time of reckoning for the both of them.

"Dean," she began again, "we need to talk. Can I come in?" She waited anxiously while he seemed to be considering her request. Trying to read his eyes, she found they were hooded against her, blocking her out.

Dean's voice when he finally spoke was husky, sounding somewhat deeper than usual, "If you insist."

Those three words sounded so clipped and emotionless that Mackenzie was chilled to the depths of her being. Her heart ached; this wasn't what she'd wanted to hear from him.

Walking into the middle of the lounge room, Mackenzie turned to look at him, not really knowing what she should do next. Her fingers became unwilling playthings as she twisted them nervously between her clammy palms. If Dean noticed her discomfort, he chose to ignore it, waiting instead for her to once again speak.

"Is this how it's going to be, Dean?" she said at last, finding the silence was too nerve wracking for her to bear.

"You're the one calling the shots," he slung at her. "You presume to have all of the answers. I'm just a mere male who had the misfortune to get caught up in your web."

Dumbfounded, Mackenzie just stared at him, cut to the quick by his remarks, which had stung and hurt her to the very core of her being, but they also served to free her from her self-imposed prison of blame.

"Hang on a minute, I came over here with my heart in my hands, hoping you'd forgive me for being so impulsive, but I'm not the one who got a phone call, telling me I was about to become a father. I'm not the one who—" Dean raised a forefinger to her, forcing her to stop her rambling tirade. She stopped talking in mid-sentence, more from shock than anything else. She certainly wasn't afraid of him even though he was slowly advancing towards her.

"Good lord, listen to yourself," he flung at her savagely. He was standing immediately in front of her now, and Mackenzie could see his chest heaving as the anger coursed through him. "You've set yourself up as my judge and jury without giving me a chance to defend myself either way. You went running off half-cocked, presuming all the while that I was guilty." While his brown eyes bored into her, his dark brows had become a grim line slashed across his forehead, letting her know in no uncertain terms that he considered her hasty retreat to be a desecration of their love.

"Well, seeing we're on the subject," Mackenzie rebelliously threw caution to the wind and asked him, uncaring now of the consequences that her outburst might produce, "are you guilty?"

"Of what?" Dean's hands were balled into tight fists as he valiantly tried to control the exasperation he was feeling towards Mackenzie at the moment. He grunted in irritation, knowing he was close to the end of his tether as she stood defiantly glaring up at him. He continued, grinding his words out through clenched teeth, "Of loving you, of being foolhardy enough to believe you loved me too?"

His answer threw her, but she realised sadly that he'd side-stepped her question. Was this his way of professing his guilt to her of his impending fatherhood? This constant arguing was getting them nowhere, but her own frustrations at not getting the answers she wanted was grating at her already overtaxed nervous system.

"A simple yes or no would have done," she shot at him, squaring her shoulders in a bravado which she was far from feeling.

Dean was silent for so long she thought he wasn't going to answer her, but she soon realised the reticence on his part not to speak was caused from anger and nothing else.

In any other circumstances, the look on Dean's face could have been deemed as comical. Stealing a look from under her lashes, she was startled to see the degree of intensity that he was bestowing on her with eyes that glittered with cold fury.

"Go . . . now," he demanded quietly, in a voice which brooked no argument.

CHAPTER SIX

So began the worst period, by far, that Mackenzie could ever remember living through. Even her grief at losing Steve didn't compare with the heart wrenching despair she felt whenever she found herself in Dean's immediate vicinity. He was always courteous and maticiously polite on any occasion that forced him to have prolonged contact with her.

On the surface, Mackenzie smiled and even managed to crack the occasional joke with the other teachers in her staffroom, but inside her heart had shriveled up within her breast. At first, she'd fervently hoped that they'd be able to overcome the argument and mend the rift that yawned between them; but as the days passed, she began to lose all hope that there could be any reconciliation between them.

On the first day back at school after the holidays, Dean called her into his office for a conference. He wanted to tell her about the charges which had been laid against her by her year twelve student.

"You'll be happy to know that all charges have been dropped against you. It seems the boy has had a change of heart after talking to the local police, something about defamation of character. Congratulations, it must be a relief for you to have that nasty business out of the way." His words sounded hollow in her ears, and Mackenzie thought he was no doubt remembering how he'd told her he believed in her innocence while she'd dubbed him guilty of a far greater crime.

"Thank you," Mackenzie told him. In all of the confusion of the last few weeks, she'd totally forgotten about the charge that had been brought against her by her former student. She rose to leave, but his hand snaked out to detain her. Her heart leapt at the unexpected contact, but she was quick to veil her feelings, lest he should see how his touch still affected her.

"Before you go, I'd like to get a few things straight between us." He sighed before going on cautiously, "It seems we're back to square one in our personal relationship, Mackenzie. Your betrayal has clearly indicated that there can no longer be any future for us. Where there is no trust, there can be no love. I have no desire to argue with you. I would prefer it if we could maintain a professional relationship while at work, at least, but if you feel you're unable to do this, then I suggest that you think very seriously about the transfer you were recently offered. Of course, what you do with your personal life is purely up to you . . . Do we have an agreement?"

Mackenzie could hardly believe her ears; he was telling her he wanted her to go. She nodded her agreement, not trusting her voice, fearing it would let her down. A painful lump had lodged itself firmly in the back of her throat, threatening to break apart her hard won composure that she'd worked so hard to establish since the night he'd ordered her out of his house.

How she made it through that first painful day back at school, she didn't know. Over the holiday break, she'd been able to hide herself away, of Dean she'd seen nothing, presuming that he'd gone away.

Walking into her bedroom later that week, she felt totally exhausted from keeping up the endless charade for the benefit of everyone at school. Not for a second would she let her guard down and reveal how very badly she was suffering. Her bedroom became her haven and her refuge, being the only place where she'd allow herself the luxury of letting go of her tightly leashed emotions.

Day after endless day, she'd arrive home, tired and forlorn; her mask of gaiety would disappear as if by magic, revealing her true feelings of bleakness and despair. She was starting to lose weight. Her clothes hung on her like she was a clothes peg, but try as she might to eat, her appetite had vanished. Her fellow teachers were all starting to express their concern, but she'd fob them off, telling them lightly that she needed to lose a few kilograms. How could she tell them that she was pining for a man who no longer wanted her, showing not the slightest bit of concern for her personal well-being?

"There must be something I can do to help myself get through this horrible dilemma," she said to the four walls that enclosed her bedroom. Stepping out of her clothes, she headed for the bathroom. A nice cool shower would help her flagging spirits. Today had been very hot despite the fact that summer was now officially over. Mackenzie could feel the perspiration trickling down the back of her neck. She hadn't been feeling particularly well over the last few days and now suspected that she was in for a bout of the flu. Some of her students had been away sick. *And now*, she thought dejectedly, *it looks like I'm going to go down with it as well.* Confirming her thoughts, she started to sneeze, sending her racing for a handkerchief to wipe her nose, which, all of a sudden, had started to run.

The cool jets of water on her heated body helped for a short while, but as soon as she emerged from the shower, her temperature started to climb once more. Fumbling through her underwear drawer for something cool to wear, she finally found a pair of red boxer shorts which were emblazoned with large white flowers and a skimpy tank top which barely covered her, but she was past caring how she looked.

She lay dejectedly on the bed, feeling the tiredness she'd been warding off all day starting to claim her. Her limbs felt extremely heavy as she drifted off into a troubled sleep where, as always, her dreams were of Dean, who always seemed to be just out of her reach, and try as she might, she could never catch his attention. He wouldn't acknowledge her presence, and when she tried to approach him, he would always fade away into the misty distance accompanied by the brunette woman who had visited him when he'd first moved next door.

Today her dream was different. Today he came up to her, but instead of showering her with the love she craved, he was very angry; and his voice, although gruff, seemed to be edged with concern. Hearing him speak to her in this way made Mackenzie feel miserable.

A gentle hand was shaking her shoulder while another seemed to be on her forehead. Mackenzie whispered huskily, not yet realising that her dream was indeed a reality. "Go away, leave me alone. I don't want you anymore," she told the apparition who stood stooping over her.

"Be quiet," Dean silenced her. "I needed to know if you were looking after yourself properly. By the look of you, my suspicions were correct. When did you last have a decent meal?"

Looking up through eyes that would not focus properly, Mackenzie regarded the man standing over her. "I've been sick," she told him feebly. "I caught a virus from my students." She struggled to sit up but was pushed firmly back against the pillows. She was bewildered to see him in her bedroom, perhaps she was still asleep. "How . . . how di . . . did you get in here?" she stammered, feeling the blood beginning to pound through her veins at the sight of him, but she was too sick to do any more than acknowledge his presence in her bedroom.

"Never mind that. Answer my question, when did you last eat a proper meal?" he repeated. She could see a pulse beating at the base of his neck, and without thinking, she feebly reached out to touch him, finding she didn't have the strength to carry out even that small feat. Her hand felt heavy and dropped limply to her side. Feeling tired, she wanted only to sleep, and then maybe this hallucination of her beloved Dean would disappear and leave her in peace.

"Cold," she mumbled to herself as she started to curl up into a tiny ball, trying to keep warm, "I'm cold."

"Damn it, Mackenzie, wake up," She heard real concern in his voice as she fought valiantly to go back to sleep. Dean shook her roughly by the shoulders, willing her to acknowledge his presence in the semi-darkened room.

"Too tired," she muttered, but even as she whispered the words, she could feel herself being drawn out of the cocoon of sleep that had enveloped her.

"That's better," Dean told her as he gently lifted her head to place another pillow beneath her.

"Why are you here?" she asked him, unaware that she'd asked him a similar question not five minutes ago.

"To feed you," came his short reply. "Will you be alright if I leave you to go to the kitchen?"

"I'm not hungry," she told him shortly.

"That's my Mackenzie," he countered, smiling grimly down at her, "fighting me even from the depths of sickness."

"I'm not sick," she threw at him, confused by his term of endearment. Perhaps she was still asleep and this was someone's idea of a cruel joke.

"Okay, anything you say, just don't go back to sleep before I come back or you'll be sorry."

Mackenzie stared at him as he made his way out of the room, not being able to comprehend what was going on. Was he here out of a misguided sense of chivalry? If that was the case, she'd put his mind at rest. The last thing she wanted was for him to have to minister to her because of the feelings they'd once shared.

Slowly swinging her legs over the side of the bed, Mackenzie was assaulted by a wave of dizziness, which hit her with tremendous force, giving her no choice but to wait until she felt strong enough to try again. This time, aided by the strength of the wall for support, she made her way towards the kitchen where she could hear Dean moving around. The smell of eggs cooking filled her nostrils, and it was all she could do not to be sick.

"You don't have to do this," she told him feebly, using the kitchen wall to prop herself up, feeling very strange all of a sudden, for her head had started to spin, and she was finding it difficult to focus her attention on him, in fact, on anything at all.

"Hey, what are you doing out of bed?" he admonished her as he swung around to see her standing watching him.

"I wanted to . . . to tell you . . . not . . . oh," Mackenzie wailed as her head began to spin even faster. She had to grab onto something before she lost her balance completely.

Dean was beside her in an instant, holding her easily against himself. "Damn it, Mackenzie, I told you to stay in bed. You're one of the most stubborn women I've ever met." Picking her up as if she was a piece of flotsam blowing on the wind, he proceeded to carry her back to her bedroom.

Tears sprang to Mackenzie's eyes as she picked up on Dean's tone of voice. She hadn't wanted to make him angry; she'd only wanted to tell him there was no need for him to look after her.

"I'm sorry," she told him dejectedly, hoping he'd believe her. Their relationship might be null and void as far as he was concerned, but she still loved him deeply with an all-consuming passion that wouldn't let her forget him.

Ignoring her apology, Dean laid her gently onto the bed. Seeing her there brought back memories which he'd been trying to erase from his troubled mind. She looked so fragile, so pale. He gazed down at her near naked form and noticed not for the first time that she'd indeed lost a considerable amount of weight. Her body which had always been so vibrant and alive looked gaunt and hollow, a clear sign which indicated to him that she wasn't looking after herself. He felt a twinge of guilt, knowing that he was responsible for Mackenzie's unhappiness. He'd been unnecessarily cruel and heartless, but then he'd been hurt by her apparent rejection of him, feeling betrayed.

Sitting on the side of the bed, making sure she was comfortable, he saw the tears which she was trying to hide and felt all sorts of a mongrel, knowing he was the cause of her despair.

"Please don't cry, Mackenzie," he said, soothing the damp hair away from her face, repeating the simple gesture several times, feeling the heat that was emanating from her fevered brow as he did so.

"I'm not c . . . crying," she hiccupped as she tried to stop the flow of fresh tears falling from her already tear-stained face.

Smiling grimly, Dean could feel the magnetic pull that Mackenzie still had over him starting to stir within him. Impulsively, he bent down and softly pressed his lips to hers, feathering her mouth with a quick succession of light kisses. "That's for lying to me," he told her gently as he gazed down at her. He added almost against his will, feeling the words were being torn from him, "We're still travelling over very rocky ground, aren't we?"

He left the room before she could conjure up a suitable answer, returning a few minutes later with a plate of scrambled eggs and a glass of orange juice, which he set down on a tray in front of her.

Mackenzie looked up at him defiantly through flu-glazed eyes that refused to focus properly. "I told you I'm not hungry." She knew she was being petulant and ungrateful, but it was her only defense against his nearness. Her traitorous body, even in the throes of sickness, was letting her down and had started to tingle, making her slight frame shudder as she looked up at him.

"Be quiet." his chocolate brown eyes were fixed on her as if she was a bothersome child. "Come on, sit up and eat, then I promise to let you sleep." He lifted her like she was a rag doll which had lost most of its stuffing.

"Eat!" he said shortly, pointing to the food which he now placed on her lap, watching as she obediently spooned some food into her mouth. When she'd eaten a few mouthfuls, he seemed satisfied and walked out of the room, telling her he'd be in the kitchen if she needed him.

If she needed him, she thought to herself sadly. She needed him, but he didn't need her any longer. The thought saddened her and fresh tears sprang unbidden to cloud her already blurred vision.

She ate as much as she could manage, but the plate still looked virtually untouched. She'd taken a few sips of the juice but found the liquid to be bitter on her palate.

The house seemed quiet, making Mackenzie think that Dean had gone home, leaving her to fend for herself now that he'd played the part of the Good Samaritan. Shuffling slowly out of bed, careful not to spill any of the food, she was assailed by another wave of dizziness and was forced to sit quietly on the side of the bed until it had passed. Finding her feet, she found she had to stand still until she had her balance, and only then did she start to navigate her way towards the kitchen at the other end of the house, precariously holding the tray of food in hands that weren't quite steady.

The hallway seemed endless, but she was determined to get the tray into the kitchen, knowing she could always collapse into a lounge chair if the need arose. She only made it a few steps out of her bedroom when disaster struck. In her weakened condition, she tripped over one of her shoes which sent her sprawling head first down the length of the hallway. She was aware of two things happening at once in quick succession. First, she felt an acute, sharp pain in her wrist which took the brunt of her fall because she instinctively put out her hand, trying to save herself from her headlong flight.

Dean seemed to appear out of the very air which surrounded her, mouthing an explicit expletive as he quickly took in the scene before him.

"Mackenzie, sweetheart, are you alright? Can you move? What have you done to yourself?" She could hear the raw anguish emanating from his strong voice as he knelt down beside her to gauge the exact nature of her injuries.

"I thought you'd g . . . gone," she answered brokenly, trying unsuccessfully to gain some semblance of control over her battered body. Her left wrist had started a painful throbbing, and there was an unnatural lump and swelling, which told its own fatal tale. The contents of the tray were strewn across the floor, shattering the glass on contact, some of which had cut deeply into her side, giving her a nasty gash which was now freely oozing blood all over her before finding its way to the floor, where it was forming a large red puddle, giving testimony to the deepness of the cut.

"I was trying to get the tray to the kitchen." It seemed important that she explain to him why she'd disobeyed his wishes. "I thought you'd gone."

"Okay, we'll talk about that later." he was more concerned with the extent of her injuries, blood was staining the floor at an alarming rate, which indicated the laceration in her side was in need of immediate attention.

"I'm sorry," she whimpered, "I'm very sorry for being such a nuisance to you." She had started to shake uncontrollably while her teeth chattered, probably from shock, as she lifted her left hand to her face, forgetting momentarily that it had been injured. She groaned as a sharp pain shot through her wrist, turning her already pale face to a ghostlike pallor.

Pulling his shirt over his head, Dean swiftly placed it against her side, trying to stop the flow of blood. In her weakened condition, the last thing she needed was to lose more blood. Mackenzie tried to stop him but was powerless against his masculine strength.

"Your shirt," she whispered feebly as she watched the red liquid greedily claim the finely woven fabric.

"Leave it," he ground out and then added softly, "You can buy me another one, when you're feeling better."

"Yes," she whispered softly, feeling very tired now, wanting only to sleep. "Dean, take me to bed."

Looking momentarily stunned, he gazed down at her upturned face. Bleak, brown eyes searched hers as he tried to comprehend the meaning behind those innocently spoken words. Common sense finally prevailed as he quietly told her, "The only place you're headed for is the hospital. You need stitches in your side, and if I'm not mistaken, your wrist is either broken or very badly sprained. That's without even considering all of the other stuff. Mackenzie," he looked intently down at her as he said, "I'm going to have to move you. It might hurt your wrist, but I'll be as careful as I can. Do you trust me?"

She nodded her agreement. She was feeling so very tired and weak, but at least her trembling had all but stopped. Dean was so very gentle as he carefully maneuvered her onto her shaky legs, his arms formed a perfect safety net when she stumbled slightly and would have fallen. Standing passively against him, she rested her weary head against his supportive shoulder, loving the strength that emanated from his tall frame. Her face was pressed into the nape of his neck, giving her an excellent opportunity to press her lips softly against him. She savoured the virile male scent of him, breathing in deeply, filling her lungs, knowing she was stealing something which was no longer hers to take. She borrowed his strength as he slowly guided her towards the divan while trying to keep the cut in her side covered lest it should start bleeding again.

Once having settled her onto the divan, Dean told her to stay put, a request she was only too happy to follow, for she didn't possess the strength to do anything else. Watching him through eyes that were mere slits, she noticed that he was covered in blood. It was on his hands, smeared over his chest and face, but she was powerless to do anything about it. She would have liked to offer to wash it from his body, but she knew she'd be rejected in much the same way as he'd finally rejected her love.

She was having trouble keeping her eyes open, but she wanted to look at him for as long as she could, knowing that once this moment was over, she'd have to again revert to stealing covert glances of him from a distance while pretending to everyone around her that she didn't care for him.

She was mesmerised by the sight of him, noticing not for the first time how that errant dark blonde lock of hair fell over his forehead as he ran his free hand erratically through his hair as he listened intently to the voice on the other end of the phone. His glance turned to her as he once again spoke, and Mackenzie was treated to the lift of an inquiring eyebrow and a quick wink followed by a fleeting smile before his attention was once again claimed.

Finding it was useless trying to stay awake, Mackenzie closed her eyes, giving up the fight which her body had been waging against her. Sleep would be the victor this time.

She was vaguely aware of Dean walking across the room and kneeling down on the floor next to her because his voice seemed very close to her head.

"Mackenzie," he whispered softly, "It won't be long now."

Murmuring something unintelligible, even to her own ears, she slipped deeper into the calming depths of sleep. Dean had grasped her good hand in one of his, bringing it up to his mouth to cover the palm with soft featherlike kisses, which caused a wave of goose bumps to travel over her body, but she was unable to open her eyes.

"Go to sleep now, sweetheart. It's alright. I won't leave you, you're safe," his whispered words of comfort had the desired effect on her fevered mind and pained body, but there was something she needed to tell him. She needed to tell him that she was sorry for not believing in him, but most of all, she wanted him to know she loved him so very much.

Deep sleep was on the verge of claiming her totally as she whispered softly, "I'm sorry. I still love you."

She felt one of his strong hands gently brushing her forehead while the other continued to hold her uninjured hand to his mouth where he bestowed light kisses onto her palm.

"Ssshh," he told her, effectively silencing her. "I know." He placed the hand he'd been kissing against his brow, hating to see her like this, so defenceless. He realised she was probably not even aware of what she was saying to him. Tomorrow, when she was more coherent, it would be a different matter.

Hearing the shrill ring of the siren as the ambulance made its way to the house, Dean was glad she'd finally get the medical help she needed. On an impulse, he reached over her, planting one last tender kiss on her unresisting lips. "I love you too, Mackenzie," he told her as the ambulance attendants made their way through the front door.

Mackenzie slowly awoke to the sounds of hospital life as menial duties were carried out all around her. She felt like she'd been run over by a truck, and a very large one at that. Every part of her ached as she opened her bleary eyes to look around her. Memories came flooding back from the night before and, looking down at her wrist, she wasn't surprised to see her arm had been neatly set in a plaster cast which extended half way up her arm. *Great*, she thought, *just what I needed. This makes my miserable life complete.* She tried to move but was stopped by a sharp pain in her side. *That would be the great gash that I managed to inflict on myself*, she thought dejectedly. At least she didn't feel so sick; it was just possible that she was going to live through this latest dilemma.

Listening to the various sounds around her, she remembered small snippets of information as they rattled around in her head. She remembered vaguely being brought to the hospital, being seen by one of the doctors, but most of all, she remembered Dean being by her side. She'd woken up with a start, not knowing where she was, but his calming influence had lulled her back to sleep. He'd promised to stay with her throughout the night, and indeed, every time she'd opened her eyes, it was to find him sitting in a chair beside her, holding her good hand in his strong grasp. Wondering where he was now, she looked around the room, and as if on cue, he walked through the door into the room. He looked tired and washed out, but his eyes widened with unconcealed relief when he saw that she was awake and taking in her immediate surroundings.

"Hello, sleepyhead. How do you feel this morning?" he wanted to know as he made his way across to the bed.

"A lot better. I think it's possible that I might just pull through," she told him as she looked up at him.

He smiled at her deliberate joke, knowing this was an excellent sign. It meant she'd started on the road to recovery. Some of her natural colour had returned, although she still had a long way to go before her skin took on its normal healthy glow.

Starting to fidget with the covers, Mackenzie looked up into his face and told him through lips which had suddenly gone very dry, "Dean, thank you for helping me. I remember you being here with me during the night. You must be exhausted, go home and get some rest. I'll be fine. Anyway, I'm sure they'll let me go home today."

"I'm just glad I could help, but I also feel responsible. If you hadn't been trying to bring that darn tray out, none of this would have happened." His eyes looked bleak as he took in the hospital room before they came back to rest fleetingly on her face.

Mackenzie was appalled that he was blaming himself for her current state. "Don't say that! You're not to blame. You've been very kind. I won't forget how you helped me." She wished she could soothe away some of the worry lines that had settled around his mouth and eyes. She didn't want him to feel responsible for what had happened to her.

"That's what friends are for, so they tell me," he told her simply and then added as an afterthought, "Oh, speaking of friends, Jazz is on her way up. She's been very concerned about you too." He didn't add that they had spoken at length over the phone about her or that Jazz had not been pleased about her present state of affairs.

"Yes, friends," she stated matter-of-factly as she fought to keep her emotions under tight control while trying to quell a large lump which had formed at the base of her throat. Unwanted tears were also threatening to fill her eyes. She had to look away from him, not wanting him to see the effort it was costing her not to cry in his presence.

Dean's voice sounded very husky as he called her name. He didn't want to upset her, but she had to know that their situation wasn't about to change. She had to know that.

She couldn't look at him because if she did, the tears she was holding so precariously at bay would start to fall. She bit her lip, hoping he'd leave her alone.

"Mackenzie, look at me, please." Dean's voice was calm, not showing any of the turmoil that was racing through his mind.

Reluctantly turning her head towards him, Mackenzie refused to meet his eyes, focusing her gaze instead on the top button of his shirt which was undone, letting her see some of his dark chest hair as it protruded through the V-shaped opening, making her think of happier times when she'd been able to freely run her fingers through the fine silky softness.

Hours had passed since Dean's departure from the hospital. Mackenzie finally had to accept that he didn't want to continue their relationship, and given the circumstances, who could blame him? She'd single handedly made herself his judge, jury, and executioner, thereby putting to death their budding romance, all due to a misunderstanding that could have been explained in the wink of an eye, had she trusted him enough. She hadn't let him speak one single word in his own defence; instead, she'd run away like a frightened child.

Her mind recalled with perfect clarity the conversation that had passed between them earlier in the day. He'd remained adamant, standing behind his decision to end it all.

Swallowing her pride, Mackenzie had asked him if he'd take her back. "Do you . . ." Her voice had faltered, and she had to wait for several seconds before trying again. "Do you still want to try, even after the emotional roller coaster I've had you on, the pain I've caused you?" Having realised the mistake she'd made, Mackenzie wondered miserably if she'd ever be able to mend the void that yawned between them. She still didn't know the circumstances behind the ill-fated phone call that has started this particular ball rolling, but she was now willing to bet with all of her heart that Dean was innocent of any wrong doing. There would be a logical explanation, but she didn't think she'd ever find out what it was, simply because she thought she didn't deserve to know. That elusive fact would be added on to her heart-wrenching punishment along with losing Dean.

She thought he wasn't going to answer her, but she realised later that he'd been weighing up the situation as it stood between them.

"No," he finally told her flatly, trying not to let his feelings for her override his judgment. "I'd be forever wondering when our next upset would be. I can't live like that, Mackenzie, not even for love. We'd end up separating. I just think it's better to cut all of our ties now before any more people are hurt. I don't want to end up hating you."

Due to her extended leave of absence, her position at school had been contracted out to a very capable teacher who, Mackenzie was sure, would jump at the chance to have the position extended to her on a more permanent basis when she accepted the position at the little country school.

She'd made a few enquiries about renting her house, so all that was left for her to do was vacate the premises, which she did with as much haste as possible. She'd put her belongings into storage until she had clearer details about her new job. By doing this, she wouldn't have to come back to Rockhampton, thereby leaving herself free to convalesce at her parent's home. Also, to see Dean and not to be able to acknowledge his presence on a daily basis would be more than her mangled heart could bear.

To say she was happy was a gross understatement, but at least she was trying to piece the tattered remnants of her life back together. She deeply regretted that it would be a hollow shell without Dean by her side, but that was a nightmare of her own making. She only had herself to blame for the constant emptiness she was feeling.

The transition from being a teacher in a busy city high school to a teacher in a small country town was a bumpy one for Mackenzie at first, but as she became accustomed to the different way of life, she found she was able to settle down and actually started to enjoy the benefits of country living.

The people around her were wonderful, instantly taking her into their hearts. Every morning, without fail, she'd find milk, eggs and freshly baked bread sitting on her doorstep. The weight that she'd lost was starting to reappear on her slight frame until she professed to the community at large that if they didn't stop feeding her as if she was a stray cat, she'd blow up to the size of an over inflated balloon.

The school was small and serviced a lot of the properties in the district. Besides herself, there were only five other teachers, all of whom shared the workload between them, and Mackenzie found her personal resources being tested every day as she branched out into teaching areas that in past times, she wouldn't have normally ventured, finding she liked the challenge.

A few of the local land owners had asked her out, but after receiving firm, constant refusals, they left her alone. How could she tell them that her heart belonged to someone else, that in its place there was an empty shell that couldn't be refilled or replaced?

Of Dean, she heard nothing, but her love for him hadn't diminished since she last saw him. If anything, her craving for him had grown stronger, nestling itself within the folds of her heart so deeply that she could never rid herself of his memory. She'd learnt not to dwell on her yearning for him, and any letters to Jazz would be devoid of all mention of him. In fact, they were carefully orchestrated to make sure there wasn't even the slightest innuendo pertaining to her lost love. Her letters were always full of bluster and hype about the school but contained very little about her personal life except for the social niceties that were expected of her. How could she write about being happy when nothing was further from the truth? Her heart was breaking, but she'd learnt to cover it up, that was all. Any correspondence which came her way would be of a similar nature. It was as if both women were treading carefully where mention of Dean was concerned.

Sometimes receiving the occasional hastily scribbled letter from Brian, her former colleague, she'd hungrily scan the contents, hoping against hope that he'd include news of the deputy head, but this was never the case until one day, arriving home from school, she saw she had mail from her old mate.

His news was general, telling her about all of the antics that went on at a busy city high school, until she scanned the end of the letter. Blinking unbelievingly, her eyes widened in disbelief and shock. Brian had unknowingly passed on to her the very information that had always been out of her reach. The last paragraph was full of news of Dean. It seemed that his sister, Meredyth, had given birth, prematurely, to a little girl. Brian went on to tell her how sad it was that the infant's father had abandoned her so many months ago before she'd even realised she was pregnant because now, he'd never know the joys of fatherhood.

Mackenzie's head swam as she took in this astonishing piece of news. Dean was an uncle, not a father as she'd accused him of becoming. The searing guilt she'd been carrying all of these long months rose up within her, threatening once again to overwhelm her with its stinging barbs.

How could she have been so wrong? How could she have not believed in the integrity of the man she'd professed to love? She was at a loss, not knowing just what she should do, not knowing if she should contact him, letting him know that she now knew the truth behind that ill-fated phone call. If she was to contact him, she couldn't be certain that he'd respond to her heart felt plea to forgive her for her childish accusations. Her sense of rightness asserted itself and she sat down to begin writing.

After an eon of waiting for a reply to her letter, Mackenzie was finally forced to admit defeat. Dean didn't want her. She'd poured out her heart, telling him that she now knew about his sister and that she was genuinely sorry for any pain she'd unduly caused him because of her jealous tirade.

Arriving home one afternoon not long afterwards, Mackenzie's spirits were flagging. A long, lonely night awaited her, and after that, more long, lonely nights spent by herself, where she did nothing but conjure up images of Dean when they'd spent happier times together. *Perhaps that was to be her lot in life, she thought miserably, to fall in love only to lose the person she loved.* She could see a definite pattern forming, for she'd lost two men. Even though the circumstances were drastically different, it was more than she could bear. She realised she'd be willing to take him back on any terms he cared to name, for life without him had become unbearable.

The stupid thought brought a bitter smile to her lips while a fine mist of tears threatened to shroud her eyes, momentarily blurring her vision. *What a pathetic picture you must paint*, she told herself forlornly as she wiped the tears away with the back of her hand, *crying for a man who's rejected you.* She knew she was all kinds of a fool for still loving him when it was painfully obvious that he'd stopped loving her and had moved on, perhaps even to another woman. The thought of Dean being with another woman brought a cold feeling to Mackenzie's heart, and she added fuel to the emotional bonfire she was building by punishing herself even further as she turned her mind back to the fateful night when she'd accused him of having another lover. If she'd stayed and believed in him, she was sure they'd still be together.

Working in the garden later that afternoon, sparingly metering out the water to meet the needs of a few struggling plants that needed the precious moisture for their continued survival, Mackenzie recognised that the task had become a personal crusade. She wanted them to survive, telling herself that their salvation represented her own growth because if they could flourish and bloom in this hard sunbaked soil, then so could she.

Her attention was arrested by someone coming through her front gate, which always made a squeaking sound every time it was opened. *Please don't let that be anyone coming around to ask me out*, she pleaded to the heavens above. She thought she'd made her position very clear to one and all of the local Don Juans who'd beaten a path to her door. Her answer had always been the same— thanks, but no thanks. She'd actually feel sorry for any man who was foolhardy enough to partner her at the moment because he'd be getting an empty shell. Her heart was somewhere else.

Mackenzie's knees turned to water and were threatening to buckle beneath her as she turned her head and saw who was coming up the path towards her.

Dean. Oh my god, it's Dean. Her mind raced, and her heart had started to pound within her chest as she stared unbelievingly at the man who now stood only a few metres away from her. Her hands smoothed out the creases in her dress as she nervously waited for him to speak.

Of their own violation, her lips parted. "Dean . . . ," she said his name timidly, more frightened at this moment than she could ever remember being in her life. Her eyes feasted on him, drinking in his strength and his masculinity. She wanted to run to him, to fling herself into his arms, to kiss him, to tell him how much she loved him, how much she'd missed him, but she did none of these things; instead, she waited for him to make the first move.

"Well, it looks like I've come to the right place," he said at last, pinning her to the spot with his deep chocolate gaze.

Mackenzie could never remember a time in her life when she'd felt so helpless. She didn't know what to do because she didn't know why he was here. In the end, common courtesy won out, and she haltingly invited him to come inside for a much-needed cup of coffee.

To ask him why he was here seemed silly, but since he wasn't offering any logical explanations to account for his unexpected arrival on her doorstep, she had to know.

Her voice sounded tense and slightly unnatural as she asked him casually, "What brings you out here? We don't get many visitors."

Dean was looking at her, but Mackenzie was unable to read the hooded expression on his face. "I received your letter. I wanted to talk to you personally to set the record straight."

Dear Lord, Mackenzie thought, *we're acting like strangers who are uncomfortable in each other's presence.* She wanted so very much to go to him, but there was something in the way he was looking at her, something unapproachable that kept her rooted to the spot.

She felt compelled to tell him again, lest he felt obligated because of the letter she'd written to him, saying that she was sorry for disrupting his life. She told him, "If you're here to berate me for writing to you, please don't. I felt I had to let you know, to tell you that I now knew the other woman was your sister. I wasn't trying to stir up the ashes of a relationship that has long since burnt itself out. So once again, I'm sorry. You can leave now with a clear conscience."

"And what if I don't want to leave, what do I do then?" His words had her senses reeling; her eyes flew to his face as she tried to determine the meaning behind his quietly spoken words. She found she was holding her breath, not knowing how to respond or how to bridge the gap that still yawned between them.

"Well?" he wanted to know.

Suddenly, it occurred to her that he wanted her to be the instigator in any victories that might be made here today. Or perhaps he only wanted to degrade her, feeling the need for revenge, but she knew she had to find out for the sake of her love for him; otherwise, it might be too late.

Running her tongue nervously over lips that had suddenly gone very dry, she found the courage to ask, "I wonder if . . . um . . . that is . . . would you consider m . . . marrying me?"

His answer was spontaneous. "Why?" he stated as her eyes widened in disbelief as he questioned her proposal of marriage. At least now she knew beyond a doubt that their time together had indeed past.

She willed herself to continue, knowing she had to tell him one last time before he walked out of her life forever. "Because I love you," she told him brokenly, knowing it was only a matter of time before he'd become a distant memory from her past, but at least she'd know that she'd tried one last time even if that attempt had ended in failure.

"Come over here," he commanded in a voice that brooked no argument. His face held not a hint of expression, but Mackenzie did so, still not knowing just what he had in store for her.

Almost against her will, she obeyed him, coming to stand only a short distance away from him, not understanding what was happening; but her body was responding to his nearness and had taken on a mind of its own with feelings surfacing which had been carefully hidden away, and she tried to suppress the shudder of delight that erupted within her, sending tingling sensations along every nerve ending her traitorous body possessed.

"Kiss me." Mackenzie was dumfounded at his request, for she'd not expected this of him, thinking instead that he was going to tell her in no uncertain terms that he didn't want to see her or hear from her ever again.

She raised confused eyes up to his, wondering if he was playing a cruel joke on her. She noticed that a small pulse had started to throb at the base of his neck, but still, she held herself back.

"Have you forgotten how to kiss . . . I hope?" he said simply, then added, "I'll just have to teach you all over again, won't I?" And that is exactly what he did. Mackenzie responded willingly, throwing herself happily into his arms, revelling in the rapture that instantly spread throughout her starving body like wildfire as she drank him in, not wanting to ever let him go.

"Does this mean you love me too?" she gasped for breath a short time later, as shaken, she gazed lovingly up into his face.

"Yes, you little idiot, it means I love you too . . . very much." he told her as he too tried to recover from their rapturous embrace. "I knew as soon as I received your letter that my fate was set firmly in place and completely sealed. If I hadn't been so stubborn, we might even have had a little one of our own on the way."

Mackenzie's face turned serious as she told him, "I didn't know until I got a letter from Brian, telling me about your sister. I . . . I should have known, should have listened with my heart and not my head. I think I did know, honestly, somewhere deep inside me, but I chose not to listen. I kept telling myself that I was right to run . . . I missed you so very much, but my pride got in the way and wouldn't let me come back." She gulped in great lungfuls of air, trying to catch her breath, wanting to continue, but he interrupted her.

"And then when you did gather the courage to talk to me, I was a perfect mongrel pushing you away. God, when I think of all the things I said to you . . . I'm so sorry, Mackenzie. I just want to put it all behind us and make a fresh start," he stated as he reached for her again, cocooning her within the safety of his strong embrace.

"I'll have to thank Brian for the part he played in this fiasco." Seeing the blank look she threw at him, he continued, "He suggested we go for a drink one day after work, just the two of us. He started talking about you, and I guess I must have told him about our sorry state of affairs, but somehow, I think he knew. Somehow, I don't think we fooled anyone except ourselves. I'm afraid I haven't been the most approachable person around the place lately. I guess he decided to step in and do something about it, hence the letter you got. He figured, correctly I might add, that if he could get the ball rolling again, we'd come to our senses and see daylight."

"You guess?" she asked impishly.

"Well, you know Brian. He has his own way of extracting information. I had the worst head the next morning. I think I drank the best part of two bottles of scotch. I don't remember much about it. I only know I've never been so miserable in my entire life as the time I've spent without you. I feel like I've been through the fires of hell," he admitted ruefully as he gathered her up into his waiting arms. Just being able to hold her again after all of this time was a wonderful, heady experience, one he didn't intend to relinquish ever again.

"You do look a bit singed around the edges at that," she confirmed a moment later, reaching up to softly stroke his cheek before letting her fingers move across to his strong jaw line, then down to his mouth where she traced the firm outline of his lips, revelling in the touch of him, loving the warm, vibrant feeling that instantly shot through her veins, transfusing her once more from the cold, empty shell she'd become into a living, breathing woman who felt revitalised and ready to take on the world. She felt him shudder beneath her ministrations, and her heart jumped for joy when she realised she hadn't lost him as she'd feared.

"Dean, why did you act like that before, when you first arrived?" she wanted to know.

"I was nervous. I didn't know what to expect, for all I knew you could have palled up with one of the local cowboys. I was worried that I'd left it too late to reclaim your love," he nuzzled her neck as he pulled her even closer to his heated body, feeling once again that he was now completely whole.

"I thought you'd stopped wanting me," she revealed to him, trying to stop the flow of tears that threatened to spill down onto her cheeks.

"That could never happen. I love you completely. Tell me, how do you feel about long engagements?" he asked, grinning at the wondrous expression that flooded her face at his question.

"Hate them," she told him joyfully.

"Me too. Mackenzie, I want you as my wife . . . to live with me for the rest of my life . . . to be the mother of my children. Please tell me that we can get married as soon as it can be arranged because I don't want to ever let you go again." He was holding her close to his body, and Mackenzie trembled in his warm embrace knowing she was being given a second chance with the man she loved more than anything or anyone in the world.

Mackenzie's unshed tears started to spill down her cheeks, and Dean wiped them away with a soft caress. "Oh, Dean. Yes . . . yes . . . yes," Mackenzie chanted the affirmative answer as she happily gazed up into his smiling face. She wrapped her arms around his waist and hugged him to herself. "I so much want to marry you. I promise I will never—" The rest of her sentence was never uttered as Dean brought his lips down to cover hers in a kiss that had her pulses reeling and her senses singing. She returned his kiss, happy to be held in his arms again.

Her world had finally righted itself. Dean was here, and he loved her. Together, they could plan their new life free from the pitfalls of doubt and mistrust that had so nearly destroyed them.

Mackenzie stretched herself luxuriously against Dean's lean body, loving the feel of him as he lay sleeping beside her. He stirred and threw an arm over her naked body, pulling her closer to his side. Mackenzie's mind travelled back over the last two weeks, remembering how very hectic it had been; but as she lay cocooned in the loving arms of the man who only yesterday had become her husband, she knew that all of the rush had been worth it. She loved this man and was looking forward to the life they would have together. All of their disagreements were behind them, and she looked forward to a future full of love and contentment.

THE END

ABOUT THE AUTHOR

Carolyn J. Pollack

Carolyn was born in Brisbane, Queensland, Australia. She moved with her family of 5 children to Rockhampton in central Queensland in 1989. She started writing her novels in 1988 never thinking for a moment that she would even consider getting them published. Friends who had been allowed to read her stories urged her to try to have them published and so she contacted Trafford and the rest is history as they say. She readily confesses to be being a hopeless romantic and likes nothing better than to create a happy ending for her characters.